Pathogens From The Cosmos

Cosmic Poetry of Men and Galaxies, Forty-five Years on

Francis A. Andrew

Order this book online at www.trafford.com
or email orders@trafford.com

Most Trafford titles are also available at major online book retailers.

Printed in United States of America.

ISBN: 978-1-4269-1613-7 (sc)
ISBN: 978-1-4269-3993-8 (e)

Library of Congress Control Number: 2009935802

Trafford rev. 11/07/2012

www.trafford.com

North America & international
toll-free: 1 888 232 4444 (USA & Canada)
phone: 250 383 6864 ♦ fax: 812 355 4082 ♦ email: info@trafford.com

Table of Contents

Pathogens From the Cosmos

CHAPTER 1

Death On The Space Station

Deep in worry, Professor William Brigmore strolled at a slow pace towards Manchester University's main car park. He was also not a little angry because of the way in which his colleagues had, yet again, dismissed what they viewed as his somewhat unconventional theories. "Why won't people accept the obvious?", he asked himself. "Why do they persist in deluding themselves?" Brigmore had just had a blistering row with his colleagues at a Faculty of Science meeting.

Brigmore was an astrochemist by training. He liked to balance his academic work with practical research. This made him feel he had one up on his colleagues who were mainly engaged in theoretical work. So, quite a lot of Brigmore's time was spent at the great Jodrell Bank radio telescope situated in Macclesfield around 20 miles south of Manchester. There, he analysed the molecular gas clouds in our galaxy and in other galaxies. Since the latter part of the 20th century, astrochemistry had been steadily on the ascendant as over 200 organic molecules had been identified in interstellar gas clouds, comets, asteroids and meteors. However, even by the year 2050, it still had to become a major branch of astronomy. Brigmore felt that that time was long overdue. With only one year until retirement, he was convinced that what was happening at the University would by no way provide him with the glorious end with which he hoped his career would be crowned. "At 60, I think it's a bit too late for a Nobel Prize", he mused.

As Brigmore was about to get into his car, a young female student from the University's Christian Union approached him with a leaflet and with the inevitable question "are you saved?"

Brigmore had never had any time for religion. All he could say to the zealous young student was, "oh not now love, I'm far too busy and I'm just not in the mood. And in any case I'm sure that it is in science that the human race will find its true destiny".

The young lady replied, "it is by the Blood of Christ that we are saved".

Brigmore looked at her and gave her a somewhat pitying smile before getting into his car and driving off to London. "The silly wee lassie", thought Brigmore to himself. "What on Earth are they letting into the universities these days?!"

The Director of the British section of the Anglo-Canadian-American Space Station was always a very busy bloke! The collapse of the United States of Europe in 2030 had freed Britain from the shackles of that highly wasteful and costly organisation. Resources could now be released for expenditure on scientific and technological development. The ACA Space Station was one of the many fruits of that merciful release.

Dr. Charles Kenning, the Director, beckoned his visitor to take a seat in front of his desk. Kenning was far from being a happy man. All 21 of the space station crew had contracted a mysterious sickness. They complained of influenza type symptoms – high temperature, weakness and fatigue. Within a few days they were all dead – seven British, seven Canadians and seven Americans.! The three Canadian and three American astronauts who went up to the space station to recover the bodies and investigate the environment inside the space station all contracted the same disease and died within a space of two days.

"What is so strange", said Kenning, "is that the six members of the recovery crew contracted the same disease and died in spite of the measures we took to detoxify the station. All our instruments showed that there was no viral and bacterial matter anywhere on the station. And our instruments are so sensitive that even one virus or one bacterium can be detected by them".

"It's not strange to me at all Charles", Brigmore replied.

"Bill, I know your theories about certain diseases having their origin in intergalactic gas clouds, comets, asteroids, meteors and such like, but I also know… eh…". Kenning took a deep breath at this point and continued, "that you intend to retire next year, and, eh, you would like your theories to be finally proven before you start to draw your pension".

Francis A. Andrew.

"'*My*'" theories!", yelled Brigmore, "not '*my*' theories. As far back as the last quarter of the 20th century, Sir Fred Hoyle and Professor N.Chandra Wickramasinghe developed the idea of diseases incident from space. Since then, hundreds of organic molecules have been found in space. There is very complex chemistry going on in the cosmos."

"Yes, but organic compounds are still not actual life".

"Oh for God's sake, Charles, I'm an astrochemist and astrobiologist, don't pontificate to me about what is and isn't life. And in any case the absorption and emission lines of many gas clouds clearly indicate the presence of microbial life throughout the Universe."

"Yet, after around 80 years since Hoyle and Wickramasinghe proposed their controversial theory, there still remains a lack of any corroborating evidence".

"That's because scientists have never taken the issue seriously, they have consistently refused to carry out the experiments necessary to prove or disprove the theory".

"And do I take it Bill that you are now telling us that here is a golden opportunity to prove the validity of panspermia?"

"Charles! You are wrong in imagining that this is all ego on my part. Listen to me carefully Charles, listen very carefully. Common sense dictates that if the recovery crew contracted a virus and died even after the space station was shown to be pathogen free, then the pathogens must have come from *outside* of the station. It stands to reason that the recovery crew brought in the bacteria or virus – whatever it was – from space. The pathogens stuck to their space suits as they space-walked over to the main docking hatch in order to operate the outside opening devices. More pathogens must have entered the station when the docking hatch portal was opened."

"This is all theoretical Bill. In fact, I'd say it's purely conjectural".

"Well, this theory could be put to the test. And the sooner the better. Now I'm not talking about my going into retirement in a blaze of glory. I'm talking about the survival of most of life on planet Earth."

"You're going bonkers Bill. What do you mean?"

"See here Charles. These pathogens are falling to Earth – slowly, slowly, but, falling they are! They will cause a massive epidemic that could wipe out most, if not, all life on our planet."

"That is *if* there are pathogens in space".

"Charles, if you and your Canadian and American counterparts do not at least take steps to investigate the matter, then you are all guilty of gross negligence and irresponsibility".

"Now look Bill! Don't tell me how to do my job".

"I'm not telling you *how* to do your job Charles. I'm simply telling you to do it!"

Kenning by now was quite hot under the collar. He was a proud man who did not take kindly to those unqualified in rocket engineering ordering him about his own business. Brigmore went on to remind him that the development of the sciences had, over the past century, been in the direction of convergence. A great deal of this overlap had been in the field of combining computing, robotics, genetics and anatomy to create a new generation of "robotoids"; these "creatures" were able to work in environments where it would be impossible for humans to live.

"So what do you propose?" asked Kenning.

"Would it be possible to use your pathogen detector outside of the space station?" Brigmore asked.

"Not at all possible" replied Kenning. "They are for use inside the space station only and have no means of operating in space".

"Then I suggest this: we adapt at least one of the robotoids with the pathogenic detecting equipment and have it analyse the space in the vicinity of the station. I'll bet my bottom dollar it will detect either a virus or a bacterium".

"All right Bill. All right. I suppose it is worthy of investigation. The main problem is that we will not have the funding for this project until the next grant allocation from the Ministry of Science".

"When will that be?"

"After the next budget – in April".

"That's four months away. We need every minute Charles, ever minute".

"If these pathogens are falling towards Earth, how long will it take before they land?"

"That depends upon two main factors – how far into the atmosphere they have already fallen and their size. It could be anything from fifteen years to one year. More work will have to be done before a definite answer can be given."

"Can't you just wait until the ACA is in a more financially sound position Bill?"

"This is a tricky question Charles, I won't know that until the wherewithal is available to enable us to carry out the necessary investigations!!"

CHAPTER 2

A Mausoleum In Orbit

Corporate backing filled the government funding gap. William Brigmore and Charles Kenning were the guests of Dr. Trevor Casper the Managing Director of Advanced Robots Inc.

"Well, there she is", said Casper . "Say 'hello' to Stella".

Stella was a robotoid upgraded by ARI which enabled her to fly as well as to walk

"Professor Brigmore, could you please give me a detailed plan of exactly how you would like Stella to operate?" Casper asked.

"First of all, I would like her to collect and analyse samples of air from the stratosphere. Then the same again at the mesosphere, thermosphere, ionosphere and finally the exosphere. Finally, I would like her to enter the space station and analyse tissue from the corpses of the astronauts who perished there."

"But surely all the systems in the station are down", said Casper .

"We de-oxygenated the station in order to prevent decomposition of the cadavers", said Kenning.

"Anyway, Stella doesn't depend on light and oxygen" said Casper .

"So when can she start her work", Kenning asked.

"As soon as you guys can find a plane or a rocket to get her air-borne" said Casper . "Once she is released into the stratosphere, Stella can fly on her own".

"That's easy enough, our own small vertical take-off jets can do that" explained Kenning.

The following day, Stella was released into the Stratosphere and began the first of her tasks. Brigmore, Kenning, and around twenty other scientists stood around their computers ready to analyse the results from Stella. By around 6pm, Stella had completed her analyses of the Earth's atmosphere.

"Look here Charles", said Brigmore. "You will see quite clearly from this data that the air samples all the way from the stratosphere to the exosphere contain bacteria and that the bacteria are identical."

"All right Bill, it seems you are right. What killed the crew of the space station originated from outer space. But we still need to be absolutely certain that it was actually this bacteria that was responsible for the demise of the crew and the rescue mission".

"When exactly can Stella enter the space station?"

"That's a tricky manoeuvre. I don't think before midnight".

"I suggest we all try and get some rest and return here around midnight", Brigmore suggested.

Everyone watched with bated breath as they followed Stella's progress on the monitors. She was fitted with cameras and beamed pictures back to the control centre of the London ACA mission. An army of technicians guided Stella in the most difficult procedure of opening the space station's main portal. At about 1a.m. the portal was at last open and Stella was slowly and carefully guided into the station.

Kenning shouted out this instruction to his team: "Freeze Stella now until I give the go ahead to proceed further".

"Why Charles?" Brigmore enquired.

"Because I need to contact NASA. They have control of the internal functioning of the station. We need light if we are to guide Stella from Earth".

"I thought you said she didn't need light".

"She doesn't, but we do."

When NASA had the space station lit up, the London control centre re-activated Stella. The pictures sent back by Stella presented a ghastly and grizzly sight on the monitors. Corpses were lying higgledy –piggledy all over the place. It was a morbid scene of death on that space station. Brigmore and Kenning guided Stella to the bodies of all the astronauts and extracted tissue from each one. By 9pm the results were through. The bacteria in the tissues of the astronauts showed that they had all died from the same bacteria that had been detected in the different levels of the Earth's atmosphere.

"Well Bill", said Kenning. "It seems you're going to get that glory after all and maybe even a Nobel Prize to boot".

"Even if that was what I was after", replied Brigmore, "I don't think I'll be alive to enjoy it all".

"Why Charles?", laughed Kenning, "have you got a terminal illness?"

"No, but I soon will have – and you – and billions of other people, not to mention a host of other species!"

"What do you mean? Is it falling that fast?"

"It's already in the stratosphere. And my analysis of the bacteria shows that it is encased in particles of space dust. This will increase the rate of fall. I reckon the first pathogenic patch will hit Earth sometime next year".

"What do you propose in terms of tackling this problem?"

"We need to isolate some of the pathogens, study the genetic makeup and then make a vaccine".

"I'll have to write a report of all of this to the Minister. Would you be willing to jointly work on the report and co-sign it?"

"Yes – but we should waste no time. The sooner we get working on developing a vaccine the better".

The Rt. Hon. Heather Penner M.P., the Minister of Science looked somber and serious.

"Professor Brigmore, Dr. Kenning, please sit down", she said to her two visitors as she pointed towards the two seats in front of her desk. For about half a minute she said nothing. She merely stared down at the report on her desk.

"I realise that you are both distinguished scientists and that you have gone to great lengths in investigating the mysterious deaths on board the ACA Space Station. However, your views on the origin of the bacteria that killed those on the space station are highly controversial. We have to submit your report to other scientists for confirmation."

"But Minister", objected Brigmore, "we do not have much time".

"Professor Brigmore – peer review and verification are normal procedures in science. Surely I don't need to remind you of that".

"I had always regarded Professor Brigmore's theories on the extraterrestrial origin of viruses and bacteria with great scepticism -until now", interjected Kenning.

"How exactly do you intend to proceed now Minister", Brigmore queried.

"I shall send your report to my counterparts in the USA and Canada . They will submit it to their own specialists who will decide on how to validate the findings."

"Excuse me Minister", said Kenning, "but 'urgency' is the operative word here".

"Believe me gentlemen, it's as much in my interests as it is in yours that we get to the bottom of this. There are 27 corpses lying inside that space station up there and we don't know how to recover them and give them a decent burial. Questions are constantly being asked in the Commons and many on both sides of the House want my head to roll. This is a disaster of unprecedented proportions. You know, I hope that you are both right about the extraterrestrial origins of the disease which has caused the death of these astronauts. It would take the political heat off me as I have no control over the cosmos!"

"If I may be blunt Minister", said Brigmore, "but as far as I am concerned, it does not exonerate politicians. Though I am not blaming you personally, I have over my long career as an astrochemist and astrobiologist been lobbying ministers of science and ministers of health to form a branch of medicine known as 'astromedicine'. This would have involved regular scouring of the layers of the Earth's atmosphere in order to detect incoming pathogens. My proposals were laughed at and I was ridiculed. Had politicians and mainstream scientists acted on these ideas of mine, we would not be in the predicament in which we now sadly find ourselves. Even if the verification tests are performed with the greatest expedition, I fear that what we may be able to do will be too little, too late."

Penning looked hard and thoughtfully at Brigmore.

"And another thing", continued Brigmore, "this is more than just the petty job and precious reputation of a politician, it is about the survival of life on this planet. If politicians could just see even only a bit beyond their noses then more could be accomplished in the field of science and technology".

This short minute and a half outburst represented a release of the frustration and resentment that had built up in Brigmore over the years and decades. At last he had got it off his chest. At last he had let a politician have it on the chin.

Penning merely looked Brigmore in the eye and told him that she would contact Dr. Kenning as soon as the results came in from America and Canada .

Three days later Brigmore got a call from Kenning who asked him to come down to London again for an interview with the Minister.

Heather Penner looked ever more somber and more serious this time round.

"Well, our American and Canadian counterparts have confirmed that there is indeed bacteria in space and it was this bacteria that caused the deaths in the space station. You'll be pleased to know Professor Brigmore that your theories have been vindicated".

"Oh! I'm as pleased as punch, Minister", Brigmore burst out. "I'm happy to see practically the whole human species wiped out just to prove my theories are correct."

"Take it easy Bill", cautioned Kenning.

"Perhaps you are projecting your own thumping low values on to me Mrs. Penner", continued Brigmore, "but I'd rather that my theories had been proven to have been wrong for the sake of humanity".

The Minister of Science simply remained calm. "Thank you for your most forthright views Professor Brigmore", was all the response that she made.

"What is the next step Minister?", asked Kenning.

"It is now out of my hands Dr. Kenning. The next step is a medical one and for that I will have to refer the entire matter to the Ministry of Health".

"I always knew that bureaucracy would kill this country", Brigmore said to Kenning as they drove back to ACA Space Station HQ UK . "In fact, it looks now as though it will kill the entire world".

Kenning ignoring this statement simply said, "during our meeting with the Minister of Health in a couple days

Francis A. Andrew.

time, we should have some definite proposals to put forward
to him. Let's not go into that ministry cold turkey".

The Rt. Hon. Reginald Hacksley M.P. seemed to
Brigmore and Kenning to be a bit more switched on than
his colleague Heather Penner.

"As Minister of Health, it is my duty to not only
accept what reputable and serious scientists such as your
good selves have confirmed, but to invite you to co-
operate with our teams of NHS medical researchers in
developing a vaccine for the sort of influenza that this
bacteria causes".

This almost brought tears to Brigmore's eyes. So often
he had been told that as he was not a qualified medical
practitioner, he had no right to pontificate on the origins
of diseases. Like his scientific forebear, Sir Fred Hoyle,
Brigmore always viewed the academic distinctions between
the various branches of science as artificial. In the realm
of nature there would always be overlap among them.
He also recalled what Britain 's most astute 20th century
politician had said about ministers' qualifications. Enoch
Powell believed that ministers should not necessarily be
experts in the fields over which their ministries presided.
If they were so qualified then they would have a vested
interest and represent sectional interests rather than the
people they were elected by and to whom they were
responsible. Hacksley was an accountant by training.
Had he been a doctor he would have been too proud to
ask his fellow physicians to work in co-operation with
astronomers and biologists in the field of bacteriology.
Now more than ever, Brigmore realised the value of
Powell's dogma. Whether or not Hacksley was good at
representing the electorate was something upon which

Brigmore did not feel competent to judge, but Brigmore was more than just a little appreciative that at least the Minister of Health would not pander to the prejudices and sensitivities of the medical profession.

"We suggest a three-pronged approach to this problem Minister", said Kenning. "The ACA Space Station authorities will send instruments into the stratosphere to collect samples of the bacteria for analysis. These will be returned to Earth and distributed to the biological research establishments at universities and other research establishments for the purposes of finding out the entire genome of the organism. When that is completed, it will be up to biologists and medical researchers to work on a vaccine to counter the disease which will undoubtedly break out once the pathogens fall to Earth."

"That sounds a very practical and logical way of proceeding Dr. Kenning", said the Minister.

CHAPTER 3

It Is Rocket Science

Brigmore returned to Manchester and worked in close co-operation with the staff of the Department of Biology at Manchester University . The Head of Department, Professor Walter Gilson headed a team of research assistants and PhD students in the task of figuring out the DNA code of the bacteria.

"Whatever disagreements we may have with our colleagues in the USA , Canada and else where", said Gilson, "one thing that we are all agreed on is that the genome of this bacteria is highly complex."

"I've never seen anything like it", replied Brigmore.

"Look I hate to sound pessimistic Bill, but this could take years if not decades to unravel. In fact it could well take centuries. This bacteria has the most sophisticated genome I've ever come across."

"Hell man!", exclaimed Brigmore, we only have months, not years, let alone decades and centuries!"

"What can I do Bill, I'm not God Almighty. We're all working as fast as we can on this".

Brigmore took a deep breath and sighed. "There's got to be another way; I mean some way by which this process can be speeded up".

While driving back to his home, Brigmore's mind was concentrated solely on the problem of how to speed up the process of decoding the genetic makeup of the bacteria. He made himself a hasty meal and sat down to watch the 6 o'clock news on TV. He tried hard not to keep thinking about the problem, but he could not.

"Damn it!" Brigmore growled as he rose to switch off the TV. "There's got to be a faster way. We've got to work at hyper speed".

Just then an idea started forming in Brigmore's head.

The following morning, Brigmore knocked on Gilson's office door.

"Listen Walter, I've had an idea concerning how we could speed up the process of cracking the genomic code of that bacteria."

"Go on", replied Gilson.

"Why don't we get the world's fastest computer, Speedy Gonzalez, to start working on it. The Harvard guys who developed Speedy would only be too willing to help us with this project."

"Bill", interrupted Gilson, "they already are. I thought you knew that. Even at 1,000 zillion calculations per second, the computer has still not managed to come up with anything."

"Hear me out please Walter. What I am proposing is this. We link up the Hypercomputer's calculating power to a robotoid. But – and here is the essential "but", this robotoid should have an artificial human brain. We take the brain pattern of a brilliant bio-chemist and grow the synthetic silicon neurons based upon that pattern. We install it into the robotoid and attach the robotoid to Speedy Gonzalez II. The technology has been developed and we can do it. We send the robotoid into the exosphere where it can perform its work undisturbed by any other matter which would be prevalent in the lower parts of the atmosphere."

"The technology has been developed Bill, but the law hasn't. You know that this is illegal".

For about ten years, debate had raged throughout the western world regarding the ethicalness of making a biological robotoid. It was somewhat reminiscent of the 20th century controversies surrounding the cloning of human beings. Genetic robots went much further as this involved cloning not just the genetic material of an individual but the entire personality of the individual.

Scientists had successfully applied the technique to chimpanzees and other primates. These animal genetic robotoids had been shown to have the characteristics of the species from which they were modeled on but with many peculiarities unknown to the actual species. Jimmy the monkey was the first such AGR. He swung on branches of trees and plucked bananas just like any monkey would do. However, when he tried to eat the bananas and found that he could not as his body was metallic and computerised, he would indicate what seemed to be depression. The same phenomenon was observed when Jimmy tried to make love to the female of his species. Also, Jimmy would never get up to the sort of tricks one would expect from his species such as attempting to snatch people's bags and cameras. One of the many other experiments that was done with Jimmy was to put him in the presence of real monkeys. Such was the hostility of his "fellow primates" that poor Jimmy had to undergo emergency "surgery" after being almost mauled to "death" by his cousins. Eventually Jimmy was placed in a cage by himself but this cage was placed next to a cage with real monkeys. It was observed that Jimmy seemed to show complete disapproval of the many antics of his "fellow" creatures.

Eventually Jimmy suffered a massive "stroke" and "died". But did Jimmy actually suffer? Was it really a stroke? Did Jimmy actually die? In fact, did Jimmy ever actually really live? The crucial question was this – was Jimmy actually conscious? On the side of the debate which favoured the development of this technology and its application to the human species, Jimmy was not actually conscious. Those who argued from a moral perspective were convinced that Jimmy was a consciously aware entity. Mainstream science generally remained undecided, the consensus of opinion being that more tests would have to be done in order to determine the conscious status of Jimmy. Jimmy neither ate, drank, defecated nor fornicated. His displays of melancholy in being unable to perform eating, drinking and love making argued in favour of Jimmy being conscious. However, when Jimmy ceased to try performing these functions and concomitantly ceased to display depressive moods, the argument seemed to swing towards Jimmy being non-conscious. And so the debate raged on. Until scientists could actually prove beyond any shadow of doubt that these entities were "consciousness free", legislatures around the world banned scientists from applying this technology to human beings.

"We're in a life and death drama involving the entire human race", exclaimed Brigmore. "This is simply no time to be debating the finer moral points of genetic robotoids. What is more immoral anyway – to allow all life on this planet to be wiped out or to take some sort of chance with a Human Genetic Robotoid?"

"You're right" concurred Gilson. "We need another meeting with Reg Hacksley though. He could initiate emergency legislation and get it quickly through the Commons and Lords".

"So far, Hacksley has been on our side. I feel confident that he will do something for us".

"Emergency legislation is exactly what we need", said Hacksley.

He told Brigmore and Gilson that he would however have to consult with the Prime Minister who would then have to put the proposal to the entire cabinet. Only then could a bill be brought before the Commons. And then money would have to be voted for building the HGR.

"We just haven't got that sort of time", said Brigmore.

"And then there's the amendments to legislation in the USA and Canada ", Gilson added. "The Harvard boffins are not going to give us the blueprint for Speedy Gonzalez prior to congressional approval".

Hacksley breathed a sigh as he rose from his desk "Please bear with me for a while as I make a 'phone call." Hacksley left his office.

Twenty minutes later, Hacksley returned.

"The Prime Minister would like to see you two, Charles Kenning and Trevor Casper at Number 10 tomorrow morning. Also present will be the Minister of Science and the Chancellor of the Exchequer".

"So does this mean…..", began Brigmore.

"At Number 10 tomorrow", interrupted Hacksley. "Good day gentlemen".

On leaving the Ministry of Health, Brigmore turned enthusiastically to Gilson . "The presence of the Chancellor would appear to indicate approval and that funds are going to be released.

"Don't count your chickens before they're hatched", Gilson cautioned him.

"To allow you to go ahead prior to legislation being enacted would be political suicide for not only me but for my entire government", explained the Prime Minister.

"With respect to you Prime Minister", said Brigmore, " but further delay could mean literal suicide for the entire human race".

"Well I'm afraid my hands are tied. This is a matter that does not fall within constitutional devices such as Executive Orders and Ministerial Directives."

"If we attach rocket engines to the HGR, could we not then say that it is not strictly speaking an HGR and thus get round the legalities that way", Kenning enquired.

"No", answered the Minister of Science. "The HGR is the nerve centre or the 'brain' of the device, not the rocket. So that would not get us off the hook".

There were a few seconds of thoughtful silence broken by Trevor Casper. "Could we not send the mechanical parts of the device into orbit first and the synthetic brain afterwards? If a conventional robotoid could attach the brain to the mechanism in outer space where there is no law then we should have solved the problem."

"The computer is built in America , the launching would take place here in Britain , and the brain or HDR is a tripartite research and development project involving Canada , the US and the UK ", explained the Prime Minister.

The Chancellor of the Exchequer took a deep breath. He looked around the room before saying what was on his mind. Essentially he was preparing his colleagues for an idea that would prove to be somewhat controversial.

"How about doing this? If we could get our American and Canadian counterparts to agree to transfer this technology to Russia , this operation could be performed from there".

"The disadvantage of that", objected the Minister of Science, "is that the Russians are not so advanced in HGR technology as we are. And besides, they can't afford to buy our technology."

"Also", interposed the Minister of Health, "they are not going to let us use their research and launching facilities unless there is something in it for them."

"There will be something in it for them", said the Chancellor. "We don't sell them this technology, we give it to them gratis. They upgrade their own science and technology at our expense and can take a great chunk of the glory if a vaccine is eventually developed to combat the bacteria".

"It's handing things to our competitors on a plate", said the PM, "but, as Professor Brigmore has pointed out, we are in a crisis of unprecedented proportions. What do you all say to the Chancellor's idea?"

Everyone nodded their approval.

"Fine I'll speak to my counterparts in America and Canada right away".

The meeting broke up for lunch. An hour and a half later they were back in the Prime Minister's office.

"Well", said the PM, "I've got good news and bad news. I'll start with the good news. The Prime Minister of Canada and the President of the USA have agreed to our ideas. The bad news is that the Russians want one of their own bio-chemist's brains to be scanned and used in the HGR".

"They want to take all the credit" said Heather Penner.

"They drive a hard bargain", said Casper .

"Well, I don't think we've really got much choice".

"I'll speak to my counterpart in Moscow ", Penner told the meeting, "and see what arrangements can be made."

The following day, Brigmore, Kenning, Casper and Gilson were at Number 10.

"Could you all please make arrangements with your respective organisations for leave of absence for at least one month?", the Minister of Science asked everyone. "You will be taken to a secret research facility in the Ural

Mountains where the HGR will be built and launched into space".

"And I cannot emphasise enough how top secret this mission is", said the Prime Minister. "You must breath not a word of this to anyone."

All indicated their understanding of the delicacy of the matter at hand.

"May we know precisely what the plan of action is?", Brigmore asked.

Heather Penner then consulted the papers neatly and methodically arranged in front of her.

"Speedy Gonzalez II and all the equipment you need will be flown to the Ural location by military transport plane. You will then all work on constructing the HGR. Dr. Alan Cowner, one of the members of the development team which constructed Speedy Gonzalez, will join you in the execution of this project."

CHAPTER 4

To Russia With Love

General Alexander Kuskaya was a big burly 43 year old. He was commander of the research station in the Ural mountains . He jovially greeted the four British scientists as they exited from their small supersonic jet plane which had carried them from London to the Ural base in only one short hour. Kukaya had something of the appearance of being a cross between an old Soviet style officer and Santa Claus!

"Welcome, welcome and welcome again to the base gentlemen" boomed the general.

They all conveyed their thanks and were shown by some of Santa's minions to their living quarters. After some light refreshment and rest, the team decided to get down to work immediately.

Kuskaya took the team down to the main assembly area deep underground. There, they saw the bits and bobs that would eventually become an HGR. What their eyes alighted on with awe and wonder though was Speedy Gonzalez II.

"Does everything seem to be in order gentlemen?". Kuskaya enquired.

"Yes, but we cannot begin assembly work until the Canadian and American teams arrive", said Casper .

"And not until *our* team of scientists arrive", Kuskaya reminded him and his colleagues. "It is part of the deal that each member of the foreign teams has their counterpart from a Russian university or other scientific institution."

"We are well aware of our obligations", Brigmore informed his Russian host.

"When do you expect your American and Canadian colleagues to arrive?", Kuskaya asked.

"Tomorrow", answered Kenning.

The party walked silently towards the lift that would bring them to ground level 100 feet up. When they reached the top, the members of the team started to make their way towards the living quarters.

"May I speak with you just a minute please Professor Brigmore?", Kuskaya asked.

"Yes of course General. How can I help you?"

"Do you seriously believe that this disease which killed your crew on the space station really comes from outer space?"

"I don't need to believe it General. It's now an incontrovertible fact".

"Well ya know something Professor – I don't believe it. It just sounds… eh .. well… just ….too fantastic to be true."

"Really now General. And are you a scientist? Are you qualified in astronomy, biology, astrochemistry or such like".

"No, no Professor. But I am qualified in basic common sense. I'm no fool."

"You could have fooled me", thought Brigmore to himself.

"Ya know! This diseases coming from outer space – it's eh, it's well, like believing in UFOs and flying saucers and eh leetle green men. Eh? Ha ha ha".

"Well General I never said anything about UFOs and little green men. Now, General, I would like to know when I could meet Dr. Feodora Kostkri whom I understand is our subject for the brain scan for our HGR".

"Tomorrow Professor, tomorrow when the whole team is here. She will be part of the Russian team. Ah but this idea of diseases falling from the sky – naw, naw! I just can't accept that."

"Pardon me General, but may I respectfully point out to you that whatever your personal opinions and prejudices may be on this matter, I expect your full co-operation in this project. The three Western governments who are behind the international team are paying the full costs and are transferring state-of-the-art technology to Russia free."

"Professor Brigmore! I know my duties. I was merely trying to be friendly and merely conveying to you my personal opinions."

"Excuse me General, but you are a soldier and not a

scientist. I tell you firmly but politely that your opinions on this matter mean absolutely nothing to my colleagues and I. Good night General Kuskaya!"

"Good night Professor Brigmore. And eh – watch out for the leetle green men and the flying saucers. Ohhhh haaa haaa haaa haaaaa".

The next morning the base was abuzz with activity. The Canadian and American contingent arrived and later the cream-of-the-crop from Russia 's scientists flew in to take part in this history making event.

"Have you met Alexander Kuskaya yet?", Brigmore asked Dr. Alan Cowner who had just arrived from Harvard with the delegation.

"Yes, I've eh had that pleasure."

"He's all right but he's got the IQ of a cockroach. Sorry if I offend any cockroach that might have overheard me".

"You know Brigmore, I used to work in Intelligence and one of the tactics of Intelligence officers is to act unintelligently. This way, those being spied on tend to drop their guard. So our General here may well just be acting dumb".

"Well, he's making a damn good job of it. Ten out of ten for acting if not for cognitive abilities".

"Don't underestimate him Brigmore, just be cautious in your dealings with him".

"Professor Brigmore!", Kuskaya called out. "Please come and meet Dr. Feodora Kostkri".

Brigmore walked over to Kuskaya's office. He expected to meet some crusty old academic from St. Petersburg

University or the Moscow Academy of Sciences. Instead, he set eyes on a 27 year old beauty.

"What a charmer for a scientist!" thought Brigmore.

"Dr Kostkri – this is Professor William Brigmore from England . Professor Brigmore – this is Dr. Feodora Kostkri from Moscow University ."

Kostrkri rose from her seat and walked with perfect grace and ease towards Brigmore.

"I'm so pleased to meet you Professor Brigmore. I've heard so much about you."

"And I'm so pleased to meet you doctor. On behalf of my colleagues, I would like to thank you very much for your agreeing to participate in this highly important project."

"Believe me, Professor Brigmore, the pleasure is all mine".

"As we have so little time to lose, may I ask you to accompany me to the laboratory where we can begin the scanning process."

"Yes of course Professor."

In the main laboratory on the base, Brigmore introduced Kostkri to Trevor Casper.

"The scan will take about half an hour at most, Dr. Kostkri", said Casper .

"Please take your time, Dr. Casper", replied Kostkri.

Thirty minutes later, the scanning was complete.

"All we need do now Dr. Kostkri is to grow the synthetic neurons in a Culture Chamber. The neurons will develop in the chamber according to the pattern of the scan we have just taken from your brain", explained Casper .

" I understand", Kostkri replied.

Brigmore then turned to Kostkri and said, "you know Dr. Kostkri, in a certain way, you are probably going to save humanity."

Kostkri, trying to look humble simply replied, "well, perhaps my alter ego will when linked up to the world's fastest hyper-computer. How long will the neural growth take?"

"About a week", answered Brigmore.

CHAPTER 5

Oh Dear What A Calamity!

"Well, quite literally – there *you* are", said Brigmore to Kostkri as he unveiled the Human Genetic Robotoid.

"If it's all right with you, we've decided to call her 'Feodora'", Kenning informed Kostkri.

Kostkri stared in amazement at the robotoid in front of her.

"Can she speak …or .. what?" Kostkri asked.

"We have to switch her on", Casper explained.

"Would you like us to activate the HGR now?" enquired a technician.

"No!" was Casper 's short but very firm reply.

Professor Brigmore then whispered something into Kuskaya's ear. Brigmore then consulted with his colleagues and made the following announcement:

"Would everyone except Drs. Kenning, Casper , Gilson, Cowner and Kostkri please vacate these premises".

Kuskaya, in the Russian language asked all except the senior Russian scientists to leave the laboratory.

Technicians, engineers, research assistants and laboratory workers all obediently trundled out of the building.

"I will now activate the device", said Casper . Casper held a remote hand-controlled object and pointed it at the HGR. A few seconds later and the HGR started to move.

"Do you hear me Feodora?", Casper asked the HGR.

"Yes, I hear you."

"Can you see me?"

The robotoid did not reply.

"Can you see me?" Casper repeated the question. Again the robotoid remained silent.

"It looks like something is wrong with Feodora", said Walter Gilson.

"There is nothing wrong with me?" the HGR said.

"The why didn't you answer my question Feodora?", said a somewhat exasperated Casper .

"Because I did not know that the question was directed to me?"

"Very well", said Casper . "I'll try again. Can you see me Feodora?"

"Yes I can see you".

"Who else can you see Feodora?", Brigmore asked.

The HGR went on to identify all the other people in the room that Kostkri knew.

"Who are you Feodora?", Cowner asked the HGR.

"My name is Feodora Kostkri and I am a bio-chemist and head of the bio-chemical research unit at Moscow University ".

Charles Kenning pointed to Dr. Kostkri and asked the HGR who she was.

"That is Dr. Feodora Kostkri. Her brain was scanned to create me".

"Do you feel anything?", Gilson asked Feodora.

"I used to feel, but I feel nothing now."

"What else did you used to feel and do but which you don't now?" asked Brigmore.

"I used to have sensation in my body, but not now. I used to eat and sleep but I have no need for such functions now. Until now I used to play sport, say prayers and carry out all sorts of charitable work, but now I would not perform such acts".

"And why not?" asked Brigmore.

"Because these things are illogical. They serve no rational function."

"Now Feodora. Do you know exactly what your mission is?"

"It is, with the aid of the Speedy Gonzalez hyper-computer, to crack the genetic code of the space bacterium now nearing Earth's surface and to develop a vaccine to combat illness caused by this bacteria".

"I hope that you will be pleased to perform this task", asked Gilson.

"No" was all that Feodora replied.

"Why not Feodora, why not?" Gilson yelled.

"Because happiness is an illogical emotion.".

"So you refuse to co-operate with the mission?", Brigmore asked.

"No".

"But you refused a moment ago".

"I did not refuse. I said that happiness is an illogical

emotion. I used to feel it as I did other emotions, but I no longer feel emotion. I feel nothing either physical or emotional although I once did."

"So you will go on the mission to the exosphere and work on the bacterial DNA?"

"Yes I will".

"Thank you".

"Thanks is illogical and non-productive".

"Enough", said Brigmore. Turning to Casper he said "could you turn her off please?"

Over lunch in the dining section of the base, Kenning asked Brigmore and Gilson what they made of the HGR.

"I'm convinced that the thing is not conscious. It seems that brain scans capture the logical functioning aspects of the brain but not the emotional or, dare I say it, spiritual parts of a human being", Gilson conjectured.

"The question is – does that thing truly reflect the flesh and blood Feodora Kostkri?", wondered Kenning.

"None of us know her well enough to really answer that question", commented Cowner.

"Well, the best person who can answer that query is Feodora Kostkri herself", came a somewhat tinny sounding mechanical voice from behind. The group looked round in amazement expecting to encounter the HGR version of Feodora Kostkri. But it was the real McCoy which they saw. Kostkri explained that a sense of humour was illogical but that she was pleased that this "illogicality" remained in her. She had been mimicking the voice of the HGR in order to give the others a bit of a scare. They all invited the beautiful bio-chemist to join them for lunch.

"So – is that thing 'you'"? Gilson asked.

"Only in terms of logic and knowledge but in nothing else. I agree with Professor Gilson that the contraption has no consciousness".

"You know Feodora", said Brigmore, "we expected you'd be in your room in floods of tears over what you had witnessed earlier today".

"I'm made of almost the same tensile material as that robot", said Feodora smiling. "I'm logical enough to know that I'm not totally logical and rational, so what is inside that thing is only a part of me. I'm no philosopher, but I know that even the logical parts of our mental composition are never wholly disconnected from our emotional and psychological systems".

"Many scientists, from neurologists to quantum theorists, are coming round to the idea that the brain alone cannot account for the totality of the human personality", explained Gilson.

"So, you're not upset by what you saw?", asked Brigmore somewhat concerned.

"Not in the least", Kostkri replied.

"However I do think that there could be an advantage in having a contraption that weeds out everything in the human personality apart from logic", Casper proposed.

"Why do you think that Alan?", Charles Kenning asked.

"Because, unencumbered by feelings and emotions, the device can sort of 'see' things more clearly than real human beings can. Charles when can the HGR be fitted with the rocket engines and placed into exospheric orbit?".

"Whenever you bio-chemists, astrochemists and bioengineers are ready?", Kenning replied.

"We still need to wire up Speedy Gonzalez to Feodora's brain", cautioned Alan Cowner.

"How long will you need?", Brigmore asked.

"Can you give us a couple of days?"

At the rocket launching site near the research base, Feodora stood motionless and erect ready to be blasted off into orbit.

"It's best that we switch her on when she's in orbit", Kenning advised.

"Why is that?", Brigmore asked.

"Because the trauma of takeoff might cause damage to her neural circuits".

"Fine, we'll activate her from base level once she's in orbit", said Casper .

When the time came for lift off, Feodora ascended into the sky like some Greek goddess. Chemical rockets were now a thing of the past. Nuclear powered rockets meant that any device could be easily and cheaply sent up into space.

Half an hour later when it was established that Feodora was safely in orbit, Casper and Kenning decided that it would now be appropriate to activate the HGR.

"Ground control to Feodora – do you read us?" Kenning asked the HGR.

"I read you", came Feodora's reply.

"Feodora! Are you ready to be connected to Speedy Gonzalez?" Casper asked.

"I am ready and willing", came the reply back from space.

"Dr Kostkri, gentlemen, if you are all satisfied that everything is in order, I'll activate Speedy Gonzalez", said Cowner.

Everyone nodded their approval and Alan Cowner started the vital process whereby Feodora's brain would work with the hyper-computer in deciphering the highly complex genome of the space bacteria.

"The genetic structure of this bacteria is even more complex than I imagined", Gilson said to Brigmore.

"The more information we get the more complex it becomes", Brigmore sighed.

"But surely it can't be infinite. This is five days now. I thought that an HGR and an SG hyper-fast computer working in combination would have worked it out in as many hours – in one day at the very most".

"Well, Walter, we just have to be patient."

Gilson's and Brigmore's musings were interrupted by a technician who entered the laboratory.

"Excuse me Professors Brigmore and Gilson but Drs. Kostkri, Kenning, Casper and Cowner request your immediate presence at the control centre. They ask you not to delay as there is an emergency".

Brigmore and Gilson looked at each other somewhat bemused then hurried off to the control centre to see what the commotion was all about.

"What's up?", enquired Brigmore as he entered the control centre.

"Feodora seems to have started to malfunction", Cowner explained.

"What exactly do you mean?", Gilson asked.

"The flow of information form her has slowed down and her voice messages are incoherent and garbled", said Kenning.

"Let me talk to her", said Brigmore.

Brigmore sat at the communications consul in order to speak with Feodora.

"Feodora!", said Brigmore in a tone of voice which was a mixture of firmness and sympathetic concern.

"What…wh…what" was all that came back from Feodora.

"Feodora – what is wrong? Tell me what the problem is".

"I cannot compute at the same speed as Speedy Gonzalez".

"But you have been doing so for five days".

"Not now, Professor Brigmore, not now".

"When did you notice this deterioration?" asked Brigmore turning towards his colleagues.

"Only 15 minutes ago", Kostkri informed him.

Brigmore returned to the communications consul.

"What do you think is causing this problem Feodora?"

"I don't know".

"Well, what do you feel right now?"

"I am unable to feel anything."

Casper walked over to the consul. "Listen Feodora – Analyse your internal structure and report back."

Two minutes later, Feodora sent this communication to Ground Control: "There is a temperature increase in my frame. I am around 180F and rising. There is foreign biological matter in my brain".

"Oh my God, Oh my God", Brigmore moaned. "I know exactly what has happened".

"You mean Feodora has been infected with the bacteria", Gilson asked.

"Exactly! What else?"

CHAPTER 6

UFOs

General Kuskaya presided over a solemn meeting of the international team leaders at the base's council rooms.

"What a disaster!", he exclaimed as he opened the session. "In fact, what an expensive disaster".

"We must try again", Kostkri advised.

"The same thing would happen again", said Brigmore.

"We must do something. These pathogens will soon hit the surface of the Earth", said Gilson.

"Have you done any thinking as to what alternative plan we might put into operation?", Kuskaya asked Brigmore.

"Yes".

"Professor Brigmore, will you please take the platform?"

Brigmore went to the front of the room and stood on the dais.

"Colleagues", Brigmore began. "Dr. Kostkri advised us a moment ago to proceed with another HGR and I replied that it would be to no avail as it would be overtaken by the same disaster. However, our colleague is right and I propose the same again ….but…. with this important modification: Feodora II's brain will be constructed with the strands of the space bacteria built into her synthetic neurons. This should give her immunity to the bacteria. However, we must work fast. Professor Gilson, how long would it take you and your team to construct a brain with implanted bacterial strands?"

Gilson turned to Trevor Casper. After a few minutes of muffled consultation, Gilson answered Brigmore's question.

"We would need at least a week, provided no further complications arise in the process".

That night Brigmore sat ashen faced in front of his television. It was reported that 300 people in the northern Japanese island of Hokkaido had contracted some sort of mysterious illness which, according to medical authorities, which seemed like a virulent form of influenza. Brigmore switched off his television set and sat with his head between his hands. He switched on his mobile phone and requested his senior colleagues to come to his apartment.

"Do you know what this means?", he asked his colleagues.

All looked at each other in amazement.

"It means", continued Brigmore, that the first pathogenic patch has hit the Earth. "I'm going to call the Prime Minister right away".

Brigmore had been given a hotline to the PM prior to his departure for Russia . He had been given strict instructions to use it only in cases of dire emergency. Here now was a dire emergency.

"Good evening Prime Minister, William Brigmore here".

"Hello Professor Brigmore".

"Prime Minister, I take it you've heard the news from Japan ".

"Yes indeed Professor."

"This is only a foretaste of what is to come. What has just fallen on Hokkaido is merely the advance guard of the main pathogenic formations. In order to help us to proceed with our work, I would like you to put into motion some vital operations".

"What exactly do you propose Professor?"

"I would like both hemispheres of the sky constantly scoured and the reports sent to me for analysis. Perhaps you could convey this plan to your American, Australian and New Zealand counterparts. I want spectroscopic analysis of the pathogenic formations and I want to know their height from the Earth's surface and their speed of descent. May I also request that you instruct the Meteorological Office to send me on a constant basis wind and air movements around the world. This way I can predict patterns of pathogenic fall out. If we have some idea as to where the danger zones are most likely to be, evacuation plans can be put into operation by national governments."

"How about Feodora Mark II?"

"She should be ready in a few days. However it may take some time to develop a vaccine because of the complex DNA structure of this bacteria. Until then, other forms of precaution ought to be taken."

"Could you give me some sort of rough estimate concerning the length of time it might take before the genetic code is cracked and a vaccine developed?"

"That's hard to say Prime Minister, but I hope no longer than two weeks".

On his way to the laboratory the following morning, Brigmore saw the rotund figure of General Kuskaya coming towards him.

"Hey, ya see this from the internet news", bawled out Kuskaya, laughing and guffawing as he handed Brigmore the printout. "The Hokkaido folks claim to have seen a UFO just before the epidemic broke out. Ho Ho Ho, it looks like yer leetle green men have come Professor Brigmore. Leetle green men spreading the leetle green bugs. Hoo Hoo it's all nonsense ya know Professor. Common sense Professor, common sense" said Kuskaya tapping the side of his nose with his index finger, " and that's what all you scientific and academic folks just don't have enough of".

"F*****g ignorant buffoon", said Brigmore to himself.

"How is the new HGR coming along?" Brigmore asked Casper .

"Oh that's the easy part, but Gilson says that getting the bacterial strands into the neural and synaptic material is proving to be tricky".

"Tricky but not impossible", commented Kostkri.

"How much longer?", sighed Brigmore.

"In a few more days Professor – that should be all".

"Sorry if I sound impatient Dr. Kostkri, but time is really now the essence".

Three days later, Feodora II was ready to be sent into orbit. That was the good news. The bad news was that all 300 people on Hokkaido who had contracted the bug had died. Two more pathogenic patches hit the Earth – one in southern Greenland and the other in central Argentina . Hundreds of people became infected and little hope was held out for their recovery.

"I really don't want to sound like that idiot Kuskaya", Kostkri said to Brigmore, "but in both Greenland and in the Argentine, reports of UFO sightings were reported from the infected areas just before the first influenza type symptoms appeared."

Brigmore took a deep breath and became thoughtful for a moment. Eventually he found his voice: "if Kuskaya had told me this in his usual mocking and contemptuous ways, I would have simply dismissed it. I am not a believer in UFOs and 'leetle green men', but there does seem to be something of a pattern emerging here. This is something which is worthy of a bit of investigation."

Brigmore was soon on the 'phone to the Ministry of Defence in London .

"Minister, could you possibly ask your Greenland and Argentine counterparts if their respective military picked up any unusual or unauthorised air activity in their infected zones?"

The Minister assured Brigmore that he would co-operate and hoped that his counterparts would too. Two hours later, the British Minister of Defence informed Brigmore that nothing had been discovered in the airspace above the infected zones that would in any way have indicated any sort of intrusion.

"Minister. I know this sounds somewhat silly, but I would like to investigate the UFO reports in more detail. Could you possibly arrange for me to interview by video satellite conference with instant translation facilities, anyone from Greenland or Argentina who saw the UFOs."

"Are you seriously suggesting that aliens are responsible for all of this, Professor?"

"I am not Minister, but this UFO phenomena may perhaps be connected to the disease".

Manuel Bernardos was a very sick man. He was only 26 years old but had perhaps only a week to live. Nevertheless, he was one of the few who were willing enough and strong enough to take part in the video interview. Brigmore commenced the interview by thanking the young man for his co-operation.

"Tell me, Manuel. What exactly did you see?"

"I saw what looked like a ball of light hovering about in the air".

"Could you describe its structure? Was it metallic? Did it have anything which looked like engines?"

"No - just a round luminous ball".

"Did it come lower down. If so did you notice any detail?"

"It descended to around 1,000 feet but it never was anything more than a ball of light".

"I see. So no detail was revealed".

"My girlfriend told me that she had looked at the object through high powered binoculars, but it revealed nothing. It was just a ball of light."

"How long did it remain in the sky?"

"For about two minutes."

"And where did it go?"

"Well – eh nowhere. It just disappeared – just like that".

The following day Brigmore told Kostkri about the interviews he had conducted with two Argentinians and three Greenlanders.

"There's a clear and consistent pattern emerging Dr. Kostkri".

"What have you noticed?"

"The UFOs have no structure and no detail. They are seen for only around one to three minutes and then just quite literally disappear into thin air."

"I don't see where all of this is leading us?"

"My calculations based upon wind movements, air speed, the data sent by optical and radio astronomical observatories and satellite surveillance indicate that a pathogenic patch will hit the west coast of north America – probably in the Oregon/Washington states region in two days time. I have asked the British Minister of Defence to contact his American counterpart. I have told him that I want any aerial phenomena seen in the region to be photographed and given spectroscopic and radio telescopic analysis. And I want to see the results immediately".

Three days later Brigmore had the data on his desk. He picked up his phone and asked General Kuskaya to call a meeting of the base's top brass. Brigmore told his assembled colleagues all about the UFO sightings, the satellite interviews he conducted with disease victims and his requests for detailed analyses and observations of the so-called UFOs.

"Well colleagues", commenced Brigmore. "I can tell you what the UFOs are".

Kuskaya's reaction to this was to start sniggering and giggling like a little girl. This served to very much rile Brigmore.

"I wish that bloody nincompoop would either take what I am saying seriously or get out of this room", thought Brigmore as he gritted his teeth strenuously trying not to lose his cool and put his thoughts into audible words.

"Ah! At last the leetle green men appear, eh Professor Brigmore?", Kuskaya sneered.

Brigmore could no longer contain himself.

"General Kuskaya. Would you please be so kind as not to interrupt my discourse and presume on what I am to say?", said Brigmore angrily. "I have not mentioned anything about little green men nor do I have any intention of doing so."

Kuskaya was completely unshaken by Brigmore's angry outburst. He just lowered his head and continued his giggling and sniggering.

Brigmore continued with his explanation: "I have analysed the data sent in from Oregon . The spectroscopic lines clearly show that the UFOs are concentrations of bacteria. Somehow the bacteria are attracted to each other when they reach the troposphere. They congregate into dense oval or circular shaped patterns before breaking up and spreading over the region onto which they fall".

Brigmore, using power –point display, went on to explain in more detail how he had come to this somewhat controversial conclusion.

"Professor Brigmore, could you possibly tell us exactly how the bacteria are attracted to each other? What precisely is the mechanism? And why should the attraction only take place in the troposphere? Why not at some other atmospheric level?", were the questions fired at Brigmore by his colleagues.

"I really have no idea at this stage. Until more work is done, I can only hypothesise as to what the mechanism may be".

"May we know then precisely what your hypothesis is?", Kenning asked.

"Before I postulate my hypothesis, I would like to convey to you another piece of evidence which would associate the UFOs with aggregate bacterial combinations. I have conducted some historical research which shows that prior to influenza type epidemics in the 20th century and so far in this one, UFO sighting were reported over the areas which were infected. So there does seem to be an historical as well as a contemporary pattern to all of this?"

Brigmore's colleagues threw bewildered glances at each other.

"Now regarding my hypothesis concerning the attraction mechanism in the bacteria", continued Brigmore, "my postulation is this: there are essentially two types of bacteria with different DNA base pairs. It is a case of opposites attract. The attraction process begins as the bacteria or viruses – whatever the case may happen to be at any one specific instance – enter the Earth's exosphere. The attraction process becomes progressively stronger under the force of gravity as the pathogens continue their decent through the atmospheric layers until they reach their maximum concentration in either the lower stratosphere or upper troposphere. The concentrations then attain the critical mass which causes their break-up and dispersal."

Walter Gilson slowly rose to his feet. "Professor Brigmore, may I point out to you that no such an attraction mechanism of the kind you suggest is known to biological science".

"I am aware of that Professor Gilson. I have already admitted that this explanation is still purely at the speculative level. However, in a short time I may have some additional material which, although may not provide incontrovertible proof that these UFOs are bacterial concentrations, will nevertheless lend weight to the hypothesis".

"One thing I'd like to point out", interjected Alan Cowner, "your interviewees claimed to have seen only balls of light but nothing in the way of details which would indicate a flying machine – engines, wings, portholes, doors, landing gear and such like. Yet many of the sightings over the past century have involved detailed descriptions of these objects. In fact, some people even claim to have been abducted by the saucers' occupants".

"My research indicates that most of these types of sighting have been proven to have been hoaxes. With regard to the situation we are currently confronted with, they do not correspond to pathogenic outbreaks. Only when the 'UFO' is nebulous and structureless and

Francis A. Andrew.

displaying no detail do we see any correlation with the UFO phenomenon and the epidemics."

At this point in the proceedings, Kuskaya became more giggly than ever. Between his giggle fits he managed to blurt out "are we finished or are we still waiting for the leetle green men tee hee hee hee heeeee!"

"Just one thing I'd like to ask please Mr. Chairman: could Professor Brigmore be more specific about the additional material he intends to present to us, material which he says might lend weight to his theory about the nature of so-called UFOs?".

"That would be premature at this stage" was all Brigmore's reply.

CHAPTER 7

Candid Camera

On the evening of the same day as the controversial meeting at which Brigmore had propounded his ideas about the connection between UFOs and pathogens, news came that another pathogenic patch had hit the Earth. This time it was in Tasmania and south east Australia . Five minutes after the news flash there was a knock on Brigmore's door.

"Oh come in Walter. What's on your mind?"

"Basically a couple of things Bill. First of all, theories about UFOs may all be very interesting in normal times, but they are purely academic in the crisis we now face even if they might be connected in some way to the cosmic pathogens. Secondly, your theory about the attraction mechanism is something I wouldn't excuse in an O Level biology student let alone a scientist of your standing. Now I hope I am right in presuming that you are about to tell me that there is some method in your madness".

"You've taken the words right out of my mouth Walter."

"Now what may I ask is this evidence you are going to present which you suggest may give added credence to your theory of UFOs? I know you didn't want to talk about it at the meeting. The reason I ask is that … that…I eh…"

"You mean you don't want me to make an ass of myself, is that what you're trying to say?"

Gilson took a deep breath and simply let out a long and deliberate "yes".

"Walter. I'd rather keep mum on things for the moment, but I would appreciate the loan of your portable digital X ray camera."

"What!"

"Please just do that favour for me", pleaded Brigson.

"Oh all right, very well, Gilson assented. When do you want it?"

"As soon as possible".

"Would tomorrow morning be all right?"

"That would be just fine".

The main laboratory was a constant hive of activity. Feodora II was kept under round the clock surveillance.

"Luckily we didn't have to start right from scratch with Feodora II", Walter Casper explained to Brigmore. "We managed to feed into her systems the information we got from Feodora I before she went belly up."

"I don't want to sound unduly optimistic", said Cowner, but if Feodora II doesn't get 'sick' with the flu as did Feodora I, we should have the entire genome of the bacteria worked out in a week and a vaccine ready a week after that".

"Even if Feodora II 'dies' of the flu, we can feed the data from Feodoras I and II into a Feodora III and so on until the final Feodora hits the jackpot", explained Charles Kenning.

"Hopefully all that won't be necessary", commented Gilson. "We are just keeping our fingers crossed that the bacterial strands that Feodora II was fitted with will give her immunity from any pathogenic assaults".

Brigmore noticed Feodora Zoskri working on her own in another part of the laboratory. He very discreetly approached her.

"I know you're busy Feodora", said Brigmore to the young bio-chemist, "but could I have a word with you?"

"Yes of course", responded Feodora obligingly.

"Feodora, how long have you known General Kuskaya?"

"Not very long. I first met him at the briefing session before assuming my duties here".

"And what was his demeanour like at that meeting? Was it different to the way it is now?"

"You know Professor Brigmore, I am classified as a government employee and General Kuskaya is my boss. It really does not behoove me to talk about my superiors behind their backs".

"I promise you Feodora that what you say will be completely off the record".

"I've noticed a complete change in him."

"In what way?"

"At the briefing, he was completely rational, sensible and professional. He seems to have undergone a complete personality change. Now I do not claim to know him very well, but these are my observations for whatever they may be worth. Also I find him to be very reclusive. I never see him eating, drinking or socialising."

"I see. I see. Thank you Feodora".

At 3pm, Brigmore asked Kuskaya to issue a communiqué for a meeting of senior scientific staff.

"No problem, no problem", said Kuskaya over the phone. "Ah my second in command, Colonel Boris, will chair the meeting".

"On no General!", said Kuskaya. "We must have the top man for this meeting".

"Why? Why?!! It just makes me giggle."

"Well General, at this meeting, there will be a major announcement concerning a big discovery. And it's so secret that only a select few may be present, I mean only a small number of hand-picked top brass can attend. Second best is just not good enough. You yourself must come", said Brigmore appealing to Kuskaya's bloated ego.

At the meeting, Charles Kenning had this question for Brigmore:

"While your theory of UFOs being conglomerations of bacteria sounds quite plausible Professor, there is still one problem that seems to have been overlooked – what exactly makes the bacteria light up?"

"At the moment I cannot say for sure but it could be caused by the presence of magnetic particles within the bacteria".

Kuskaya, who had been quiet until now, started to get his usual fits of the giggles.

"Where would these metallic particles come from and how would the bacteria capture them?", Gilson asked.

"I honestly don't know", replied Brigmore. "I am merely hypothesising".

Kuskaya, managing to control his giggles, cleared his throat and reminded Brigmore that the purpose of the meeting was to announce a major discovery and not to indulge in idle speculation.

"You are right General Kuskaya, you are right. Now! My discovery is within this camera."

Brigmore picked up the portable digital X ray camera he had borrowed from Gilson. He looked into it for a few seconds and laid it down.

"Do you require Digital enlargement and projection?", Kuskaya asked.

"I don't think that will be necessary", Brigmore replied, "there appears to be a fault with the camera".

Gilson knew perfectly well that the camera was in perfect working order. He looked at Brigmore as if to say "more methodical madness Brigmore, more methodical madness".

"Could you possibly tell us about the discovery?", Cowner asked.

"As you can all see, this is a portable digital X ray camera, but with modifications. This instrument has been modified in such a way that it may be attached to an optical astronomical telescope. A similar camera was used by the observing team working with the Anglo-Australian telescope. They have sent their discoveries to me electronically. And they're all inside this camera."

"You'd better have some rational explanation for all this balderdash, Brigmore", thought Gilson to himself.

"And what precisely did the Australian observers find Professor Brigmore", Kuskaya asked.

"The X ray photographs confirm that the so-called UFOs are in fact bacterial formations".

There was a general feeling of disappointment all round the room. Everyone had expected something much more sensational than that. It hardly amounted to a "major announcement" or a "big discovery".

"Is there anything else you wish to say Professor Brigmore?", Kuskaya asked.

"No, that is all", was Brigmore's reply.

"Does anyone else have questions they would like to put to Professor Brigmore?", Kuskaya asked the assembled scientists.

Everyone around the table merely shook their heads rather despondently.

"Then I call the meeting closed", said Kuskaya.

All left the room except Brigmore and Gilson. Brigmore remained at the dais gingerly shuffling papers and examining the camera. Gilson slowly approached him. Before Gilson could open his mouth Brigmore said, "I know, I know Walter. You want some explanation for the garbage I spoke".

"Well, yes of course", replied Gilson.

"Please come over to my office".

Brigmore picked up the phone on his office desk: "Alan, could you please come to my office if you are not too busy?" Turning to Brigmore he said, "I want Cowner in on this one".

"What's up Bill?", Cowner asked as he came into Brigmore's office.

"Bill. You told me that you once worked for Intelligence", Brigmore reminded him.

"Well, in a way I still do. Once in the CIA always in the CIA. That basically goes for Intelligence organisations all around the world".

"Then Alan, I may need your help on how to handle a certain matter. When I was fiddling around with that camera during the meeting, I actually took an X ray photograph of General Kuskaya. Would you both please look at the photograph?"

Brigmore handed the digital X ray camera across the desk to his two colleagues. Their mouths gaped at what they saw on the display at the back of the camera.

"For some time I suspected that Kuskaya was an HGR", said Brigmore solemnly and quietly. "This now confirms it".

"What should be our next move?" Gilson asked. "How should we handle this matter?"

Brigmore simply pointed to Alan Cowner.

Cowner then gave his expert advice: "For the moment, play along with Kuskaya. Don't mention this to anyone outside of this room. Get on to your government as soon as possible. Inform them of your discovery and ask them to send out a couple of MI5 agents under the guise of scientists. Their job will be to interrogate the mastermind behind all of this. And I'm beginning to think I know just exactly who that mastermind is, maybe you are too – but don't breath a word, not even here".

Gilson looked at Brigmore and simply hissed out "who?!!

Brigmore wrote a name on a piece of paper and showed it to Cowner.

"Is this whom you had it mind?" asked Brigmore as he showed the paper to Cowner.

"Yes"

Brigmore then showed the paper to Gilson. Brigmore then tore the paper into tiny little pieces and threw them in the wastebasket.

CHAPTER 8

I Spy With My Little Eye

Jimmy Bradley (alias Professor Jonathon Fitzwilliam a micro-biologist) and Colin Oakley (alias Dr. Ronald Dewar – a specialist in robotics) knew absolutely nothing about micro-biology or robotics. However, they were senior MI5 agents and were experts in interrogation methods if in nothing much else. But they were not the sort of guys with whom you'd want to pick a fight in a pub. Those who had done so soon discovered that only one smack on the mouth from either one of these charming gentlemen would knock you out cold for at least five minutes. Their plane touched down on the landing area at the Ural base and some of Kuskaya's minions showed them to their living quarters.

"Would your new colleagues like to see the complex and get some idea of the facilities?", Feodora Kostkri asked Brigmore.

"For the moment, they'd like to rest. However, they will be working with Professor Gilson, Dr. Cowner and myself on a specific matter related to HGRs and the bacterial UFO formations."

Bradley and Oakley wasted no time with rest. They got down to business straight away. Brigmore, Cowner and Gilson briefed them on the happenings at the base. Slowly and carefully, Cowner began to explain to them the plan he had in mind.

Brigmore picked up the phone. "General Kuskaya. Could you please come to my office?"

"You come to my office, if you want to see me. Don't you know the correct protocol?", said Kuskaya rather haughtily.

"General! Professor Fitzwilliam and Dr. Dewar have devised a means of dealing with any incoming pathogenic material. The instruments they have are too heavy to carry over to your office".

"Well we have plenty of porters to do that job?"

"General! These instruments are classified as top secret. They should not be seen being carried around the base. General Kuskaya, I am not insulting your seniority or disregarding protocol, I'm simply concerned with the security of top secret equipment. I have to balance protocol and security, General."

Five minutes later Kuskaya entered Brigmore's office.

"Thank you for coming General. Please take a seat", said Brigmore gesturing towards the most comfortable chair in the office thus giving Kuskaya the impression that "protocol was being adhered to".

"Thank you Professor", said Kuskaya. "Now about these instruments".

Bradley slowly rose from his chair and brought over a cylindrical shaped object to Kuskaya.

"What exactly is this contraption?", Kuskaya asked.

Bradley held out a nozzle type attachment and invited Kuskaya to look into it. When Kuskaya gingerly leaned towards the nozzle, Fitzwilliam thrust it on his face and pulled a lever. Oakley, Cowner, Brigmore and Gilson pounced on Kuskaya and held him down as he struggled to try to free himself from the gas that came pouring out of the cylinder and into his nose and mouth. One minute later he was unconscious. Fitzwilliam and Oakley carried his motionless body to the adjoining room.

"Now let's call in our suspected mastermind", said Oakley.

A few minutes later, Dr. Charles Kenning entered the office. He was introduced to Bradley and Oakley in their aliases as Fitzwilliam and Dewar.

"Charles. How long have you known Alexander Kuskaya?", Brigmore asked.

"Only since I arrived on this base. Why? Is there something the matter?"

"Do you know where Kuskaya is now?"

"Well eh – either in his office or… em .. somewhere on the base."

"I mean, where is the *real* General Kuskaya. I don't mean the HGR that you made of him".

"How dare you make such an insinuation Brigmore. Where is your evidence for this?"

As Kenning stood up in outrage and fury, Bradley and Oakley moved towards him and pushed him down on to his seat.

"This is assault. I'll have you charged for that", yelled Kenning.

"Kenning!", said Cowner. "This nice gentleman here is Mr. James Bradley, and the other nice gentleman is Mr. Colin Oakley – both are from MI5".

"My God", growled Kenning, "you'd better have some proof for what you are accusing me of or I'll have the lot of you in a libel court when we get back to the UK ".

Oakley simply just pointed toward the adjoining room.

"Go and take a look", said Brigmore calmly.

Kenning stomped angrily towards the door. He peered in. A few seconds later he returned to his seat in a complete state of shock.

"I noticed at the meetings Kenning that you were the only one present who did not show any sort of annoyance or disgust at Kuskaya's puerile behaviour. When you made this HGR, you removed everything from him except his playful sense of humour. Am I right?"

Kenning simply nodded his head in confirmation. He was now completely stunned by the swift course of events.

"Now tell us who you are working for and what exactly your connection is with the bacterial invasions from space", Oakley asked him.

In a shaking and faltering voice, Kenning tried to find the words to answer the question put to him.

"We can do this the hard way if you like", said Brigmore. "These two MI5 gentlemen are really polite though – they'll raise their hats to you before they slug you one in the guts".

"There is an easier way", Cowner suggested. " If Dr. Kenning could give us the code for the Kuskaya HGR, we could play back all the memories from his synthetic neural system on the desktop here".

" Well Dr. Kenning?", said Gilson.

Kenning gave Brigmore and Cowner the code. The Kuskaya HGR's head was opened and its neural component connected by wires to Brigmore's desktop.

In a mere twenty minutes, the whole sordid story was out.. Kenning had understood all along that pathogens from outer space had killed the ACA space station crew. He had put a number of HGRs in orbit with the instructions to plot the advance guard of the main body of pathogens and to weight them with magnetic iron filings as they approached the lower stratosphere. As the Earth became increasingly contaminated, he and his corporate backers would take refuge in the space station after it had been detoxified. With most of the human species wiped out on the planet, Kenning and his backers would return to rule the Earth once the disease had run its course.

"Charles, Charles!", exclaimed Brigmore. "How could you do such a despicable thing?"

"Humanity is corrupt", said Kenning. "The Earth ought to be ruled by an elite of scientists who implement policies based upon logic. As a man who has no time for religion or philosophy, I thought you would have seen eye to eye with me on that one Bill".

"I may be a Humanist, Charles, but I am also a humanitarian. Sadly Charles, you seem to have lost your humanitarianism somewhere along the line".

"Now then", interjected Gilson, "where is the real Kuskaya?"

"Locked up in one of the old underground Soviet prison cells", Kenning replied.

"How many stand guard outside his cell", Bradley asked him.

"Two".

"Take us to him", Oakley commanded him. "Make any funny move Kenning and you're history".

The group made their way towards what looked like an old disused clump of buildings on the perimeter of the base. They entered one of the buildings and walked down a cold stone stairway that led to a row of cells. As they walked along the corridor, they saw two guards on duty at the very end of the row. They were standing watch over a single solitary cell with a single solitary figure within it.

"Now!" said Bradley sticking a hand-gun into Kenning's ribs.

"We want to talk to General Kuskaya immediately", barked Kenning to the guards.

As the guards turned towards the cell door, Bradley shot them both dead. As there was a silencer on his weapon, there was no noise created by the shots to arouse anyone on the base.

"Now, before you take this rascal back to Britain for incarceration", said Brigmore, "there is one more question I'd like to ask him." Turning to Kenning he put this question: why did you involve Feodora in all of this? Or – may it be more to the point to ask if she in fact *is* involved in all of this?"

"We need a vaccine just as much as you do", Kenning replied. "So we wanted to use her bio-chemical and medical knowledge for this purpose".

CHAPTER 9

A Much Needed Shot In The Arm

The real general Alexander Kuskaya turned out to be a very intelligent and highly educated individual.

"We have to find out just how many of Kennings plants are on the base", Kuskaya said.

"Those guards we killed will have to be relieved at some point", said Cowner. "We need to watch the area carefully to see who goes to replace them."

"Can't we find out through CCTV?" Bradley asked.

"That area is not covered due it being derelict", Kuskaya answered. "Anyway, the new guard will come at 3pm. There are a total of four guards in all."

"This time", said Brigmore, "don't kill them as we may need them for information. We want to know who exactly is working for whom".

"They are working for the Borlitsky Corporation", explained Kuskaya." When I refused to go along with their evil schemes, they … well, to cut a long story short, they kidnapped me. Kenning took a scan of my brain and created that HGR".

"Why didn't they kill you after the scan?", Oakley asked.

"If anything went wrong with the first HGR or if they decided they might need a stock of these things, then they would have to keep the original I suppose".

At 3pm the relief guards were waylaid and taken to Brigmore's office for interrogation. After some 'gentle persuasion' from Bradley and Oakley, they gave a list of all Borlitsky Corporation plants working at the Ural base. They were arrested and incarcerated in the old Soviet dungeons. Kuskaya informed the authorities in Moscow about the recent events at the Ural base. The Chairman and directors of the Borlitsky Corporation were arrested and under emergency regulations the company was immediately nationalised. The prisoners at the Ural base were taken to Moscow by the military police for further interrogation. Bradley and Oakley took Kenning back to the UK in handcuffs.

"We need to get back to the critical business of devising a vaccine before the main pathogenic cloud hits the Earth" said Brigmore.

"Yes, but before we wrap up this whole nasty episode", advised Kuskaya, "we have to find out exactly how many of Kennings HGRs there are and the precise orbits they are in. When they are destroyed, the pathogen advance will at least be slowed down and that should give you guys more breathing space for working on the vaccine".

Kenning gave Kuskaya the number and orbits of the HGRs. These were located and destroyed by the Russian military. The five HGRs in lower orbits were taken out by Russian hypersonic fighter planes, the ones in higher orbits were destroyed by ground to space missiles.

Two days later, Feodora Kostkri announced the great news. She excitedly summoned her colleagues into the base's main lab.

"We have it, we have it!", she exclaimed. "Feodora II has cracked the bacteria's complex genetic code. And not only has she done that – she has come up with a vaccine".

There were whoops and yelps of joy all around. This was the holy grail they had been seeking. This was the great moment they had all been waiting for.

"Our plan of action has to be to inform governments around the world," Brigmore explained. Ministries of health have to be instructed on how to prepare the vaccine."

"I would add a word of caution", said Gilson. "We don't really know what the effect of the vaccine might be. After all, we will be injecting people with a highly complex serum. There could be cases of serum poisoning."

"May I suggest this?", said Kuskaya. "Why don't we find out where the next pathogenic hit will be and administer the vaccine to those in the area. I realise we are experimenting with humans – but what is the alternative?"

"Professor Brigmore, have you any idea as to which part of the world the next stream of pathogens will fall?", Feodora Kostkri asked.

"In one week, central Africa will take a hit, and in ten days Alaska will have one".

"We must get the vaccine formula out to the health ministries in the African nations involved and to the health authorities in Alaska ", said Kuskaya.

"But we must set up some sort of monitoring system", Gilson advised.

"That will be the responsibility of the ministries of health and various national and regional medical authorities", Kuskaya explained.

"But we must arrange it so that the results of the monitoring are sent to this base", said Gilson. "If there should be any problems with the vaccine and the serum requires modification then we are the only ones capable of making these changes".

CHAPTER 10

A Logical Vaccine

Brigmore, Gilson, Kostkri and Kuskaya were in deep contemplation over the reports which had been pouring in from Africa and Alaska .

"Well General", said Brigmore, "it seems that we have both good news and bad news."

"What's the good news?" Kuskaya asked.

"The good news is that the vaccine works".

"So what then could the bad news possibly be?" Kostkri wondered.

"It is very strange", answered Brigmore. "While the vaccine provides immunological protection, it has an adverse effect in a sort of psychological cum neurological way."

"Could you be more specific?" Kuskaya asked,

"Those who have been administered the serum lose all their …sort of spiritual and philosophical faculties.

They look on the world in purely functional ways. They see no point in such things as religion, art, decoration, beauty, theatre, literature, laughter and such like. Their whole outlook changes. They express their support for such practices as euthanasia and abortion – and these views are being expressed by Roman Catholic clergy in many cases."

"Another disturbing report which I have states that many people who have benefited from the vaccine have suggested that the majority of people in the world should not be administered it so that world population may be reduced."

"My God, my God", cried Kuskaya, "people who are given the vaccine lose their humanity."

It then dawned on all around the table as to exactly what was happening. Dr. Kostkri articulated what was collectively understood. "People are being made into HGRs."

"Yes", said Gilson. "We made HGRs in our image. Now the HGR in orbit round the Earth is attempting to create humans in its image".

"We have to contact Feodora II and find out more", Kostkri suggested.

At the communication and command centre of the base, the team readied themselves to interrogate Feodora II. They informed the HGR of their alarm over the psychological changes in people who had been administered the vaccine.

"Could you confirm what you mean by such terms as 'spiritual', 'religion', 'art', 'drama' and 'beauty'?", the HGR requested.

Feodora II was sent all the information on all the world's religions which were stored on the Digital Internet Grid. In the same way she was supplied with data on every aspect of every subject in the arts and humanities.

"Feodora! How long will it take you to process all this information", Brigmore asked.

"About one month", was the reply.

"Damn, damn and double damn!!", screamed Brigmore. "We haven't got that long."

At this point Alan Cowner walked in and asked what all the commotion was about.

"If only you had brought me in on this. I know I'm not an astronomer or an astrobiologist or astrochemist, but I do know a little bit about computers". Cowner was somewhat miffed about having been excluded from the inner circle on this occasion.

"Please continue, Dr. Cowner", said Kuskaya.

"Feed the same information to Feodora II again – but this time, through Speedy Gonzalez!"

"Alan, we did not mean to exclude you", Brigmore apologised. "We thought that everything automatically went through SG."

"I'm not suffering from bruised ego", Cowner protested, "but the world's fastest hyper-computer is up there in space and I am its chief architect. There are two ways in which information can be sent to Feodora: directly to her neural base, her 'brain' if you like. That is doing things the long, slow way. However, through SG, you'll get the results in a fraction of the time. Speedy Gonzalez is not attached to her as an adornment to make her look pretty you know".

Francis A. Andrew.

"OK", said Gilson. "How long will it take her to process the information through SG".

Cowner smiled a superior smile on all his colleagues: "About half an hour", he softly replied.

Half an hour later, Brigmore and his team were all ears for Feodora II.

"Well Feodora?", said Brigmore.

"The information which you have fed me and which falls under the categories of arts, humanities and divinity are illogical. I cannot deal with them."

"Feodora", continued Brigmore, "you are to obey instructions whether or not you consider them to be logical".

"It is impossible for me to do that".

"Why?"

"Because I am possessed only of logical and computational faculties".

"We want you, Feodora, to devise a modified vaccine which will not interfere with the eh the em eh non-logical faculties of the human mind".

"I am not equipped to deal with abstract matters".

"And why not?" interjected Gilson.

"I have already explained why, Professor Gilson".

"We are not asking you to dabble in abstract thinking, Feodora", Gilson continued, simply alter the serum so that non-logical functions may be retained by those to whom the vaccine is administered".

"Again impossible. My neurological circuitry is partly comprised of strands of the bacteria now falling upon the Earth. It is the nature of this bacteria to attack the parts of the brain which do not correspond to logic. That is why I live and Feodora I died".

"But Feodora was totally logical", objected Cowner.

"No, she was not. She still had residual non-logical elements in her neurological make-up, although, these were never actually demonstrated".

"And what precisely makes you so different?", Kuskaya asked.

"When I was constructed I had exactly the same make-up as Feodora I. However, when the bacterial strands were implanted in my neurological system I gained immunity but the residual non-logical faculties were destroyed. This is precisely what is happening to those on Earth who are being inoculated against the space pathogens. Those who are not inoculated die because in a pre-inoculated condition the human brain consists of a large component of non-logical faculties".

"I've heard enough", said Brigmore as he walked away from the communications consul. "We are caught between the Devil and the deep blue sea. The vaccination basically allows us to save only a small fraction of each human being."

"It allows humans to function as mere organisms but not as complete and total human beings", Casper noted.

"So what do we do?", asked Kuskaya. "Do we go ahead with the vaccination programmes or not?"

"Well, better a fraction of a human being than a dead one I suppose, said Kostkri.

"There has to be a more satisfactory solution than that", said Brigmore gritting his teeth, 'there just *has* to be".

"But what is it Professor, what is it?"

"That's the million dollar question", said Cowner.

That evening Brigmore once more went into one of his depressive moods. He thought and thought and thought and thought but could find no way out of the appalling dilemma. Generally, Brigmore was not what might be called a 'cursing and swearing' man. He would sometimes let out the odd 'F' and 'B' when he was under pressure, but only on very rare occasions. That night, Brigmore felt himself to be under severe pressure. The tension within him had built up to such a crescendo that that rare occasion presented itself once more.

"Chrrrrisst, Christ", he burst out as he banged his fists on the table. "Bloody hell, oh bloody hell……what can I do".

This outburst served to relieve the tension which had got such a terrible hold on Brigmore. As Brigmore came to his senses, as he slowly gained his calm, as his fevered mind cooled down, he realised that something was starting to dawn on him. Often, the human mind makes involuntary connections based on the spur of a moment's stimuli. It had taken a long time for Brigmore to admit to himself that it was the idiot HGR version of Kuskaya that had got him to look into the connection between UFO phenomena and extraterrestrial pathogens. Now, Gilmore had to make another painful admission to himself: the 'silly wee lassie' who had once told him that 'it is by the blood of Christ that we are saved' may have said something with a significance way beyond what she could ever have imagined and as far beyond what Brigmore himself could ever have imagined at the time. Things started to come together in Brigmore's mind. What he needed now was a plan of action.

CHAPTER 11

All Roads Lead To Rome

Brigmore was sitting in Kuskaya's office. Kuskaya was looking extremely thoughtful.

"How can this Professor John Durking have come up with an alternative vaccine so quickly?", Kuskaya asked.

"He was awarded the Nobel Prize for Medicine a few years ago. He is the world's greatest medical micro-biologist".

"But he is not a hyper-computer Professor Brigmore".

"Well, we are in a desperate situation, General. We have to listen to what he says. At least we have to listen."

"What exactly does your friend have in mind?"

Brigmore hesitated for a moment. He had to think carefully yet fast as to how to answer the General's question. "It's was too complex to explain over the 'phone. I have to see him in person".

"Very well. I'll have a plane ready for you tomorrow morning to take you to London ."

Professor John Durking listened carefully and attentively as Brigmore related everything that had happened at the base over the past few months. The plan that Brigmore had in mind to deal with the crisis raised Durking's eyebrows.

"I'm not too happy with your telling this General that it is all my idea", said Durking.

"I had to find some legitimate reason for commandeering a plane", replied Brigmore.

"All right, I understand".

"What do you think of my idea? We could give it a try. I know you're not Roman Catholic but you are a practicing Christian. I thought you might be sympathetic to my idea."

"I'm Church of England, to be exact. Anyway, Brigmore, if you think it's a good idea, why shouldn't I? After all you're the atheist. It's astonishing that you would have come up with such a bizarre idea. So how do we make the first move in all of this?"

"I've arranged a meeting for tomorrow with Cardinal Orivietti, the Papal Nuncio to the UK . The meeting is for 3pm at the Nunciature in London ."

"You know gentlemen, if it were not for the fact that the world faces impending doom and that you both are outstanding scientists I would dismiss your most extraordinary request out of hand. However, I plan to co-operate with you and to beseech the Holy Father to grant you your request."

"Thank you, Your Excellency", said Brigmore.

"How long should this entire process take, Your Excellency", Durking asked.

"I hope no more than two days. First I will convey your request to the Cardinal Secretary of State at the Vatican who will then inform the Pope. We can only hope and pray that His Holiness will act promptly and positively".

Two days later, Brigmore received a call from the Nunciature that his and Durking's request had been approved by the Pope and that both men should make their way to Rome as soon as possible. They wasted no time and were in Rome that very afternoon. In the evening they were back in London having got exactly what they had wanted. Durking's laboratories started working on the new serum. It was ready in only three days.

"Quite simply Durking, how do we announce this to the world without appearing to be prime candidates for the nuthouse?"

"We could say that we have come up with a modified serum; one that does not affect the areas of the brain which deal with abstract thought processes. If it works, we'll reveal all at some appropriate future time".

"And if it doesn't?"

"We'll tell all nevertheless. For if it doesn't work, we're finished as a species anyway."

"My calculations show that the next pathogenic patch will fall in northern Australia . It will hit in about one week's time."

"Then we have to get the new vaccines out there as fast as possible."

"I'll organise all this from the Ural base once I get back to Russia .. In the meantime, I'll make arrangements with the Minister of Defence to get the batch of vaccines your laboratory has produced out to the Urals."

"Welcome back, Professor Brigmore", said Kuskaya greeting Brigmore as he descended from the small hypersonic nuclear powered plane. "I do hope your trip was successful."

"Thank you General. It is good to see you again. I can't really say that the new vaccine is a success until we try it. The next pathogenic patch is due to hit northern Australia . So we need to be moving pretty pronto in terms of getting the vaccines out to them."

"In exactly what way does this vaccine differ from the previous one?"

"Let's get our senior colleagues together and I'll give a collective explanation".

Half an hour later, Zostkri, Casper , Gilson and Kuskaya were assembled in Brigmore's office. Brigmore commenced his explanation:

"Professor John Durking, an eminent medical microbiologist has developed a serum which in theory at least should prevent the loss of certain neurological functions when administered as a vaccine."

"How exactly has he done this?", Zostkri enquired.

"He has identified a sub set of genes which are responsible for abstract thought. These have been grafted onto the main genetic material of the serum?"

Gilson started his eyebrow raising again, but he had the prudence to keep his mouth closed. By now, he had got used to his colleague's methodical madness!

"However, we do not have time to discuss the finer scientific points of the vaccine", Brigmore continued. "General Kuskaya – I want a hotline to the Australian Minister of Health immediately".

Brigmore and Kuskaya made their way over to Kuskaya's office. Kuskaya picked up his phone and dialed a series of numbers and eventually got through to Terrence Charner the Australian Minister of Health. The Minister did not turn out to be as co-operative as Brigmore would have liked.

"You're using the Australian people as guinea pigs, Professor Brigmore", said Charner angrily.

"Mr. Charner! I do not control the pathogenic formations. My calculations show that one of these is due to hit Australia in a week's time"

"How can you be so sure your new vaccine will work?"

"I can't".

"You can't!"

"It would not only be unscientific but totally irresponsible of me to give such a definite affirmative answer at this stage."

"Your new vaccine might even be worse than the previous one for all we know".

"Correct Minister. But I'm not forcing the vaccine on you. I'm simply telling you that a pathogenic cloud is on its way to your country. I'm offering you the best we've got so far. Take it or leave it Minister – the choice is yours. If you refuse – fine. I'll find out where the next pathogenic shower will fall and make my offer there. For the moment we only have limited quantities of the vaccine – the trial batch which was produced in Oxford and flown out here to the Urals is all that exists in the entire world and we're offering that one and only batch to you, Mr. Charner".

Brigmore's firmness had a softening effect on Charner.

"All right Professor Brigmore. I'm sorry if I sounded a bit harsh. I'll accept your kind offer."

"Fine, Mr. Charner. I'll arrange to have the vaccine flown out to you hypersonically by Russian military transport planes. You should receive these tomorrow".

The vaccines were flown out to northern Australia . The government at both federal and state level organised a mass immunization programme in the territory. The pathogenic cloud eventually arrived and showered its genetic material over northern Australia . Those who had been vaccinated showed neither symptoms of disease nor loss of mental faculties. The Australian government declared the programme a resounding success.

"Well, congratulations old man", said a beaming Gilson as he walked into Brigmore's office.

"Wonderful, wonderful", cried Feodora Kostkri who had accompanied Gilson to the office. "But Professor, we need to know the exact method for producing this serum so that it can be mass produced for worldwide distribution. We have to do this before the main genetic storm hits the entire Earth."

"We cannot use just any blood or any DNA", Brigmore explained. "We must use the template Professor Durking has in his laboratories in Oxford ."

"How can that possibly be?", Gilson asked.

"As I said before Walter, there is no time to discuss the academics of the vaccine now".

"Then how can the vaccine be mass produced in time to save humanity from the disaster that is coming upon it?", Kostkri hysterically blurted out.

"I have been in constant communication with John Durking. His plan is to send copy templates to every single country in the world with instructions on how to prepare the vaccine from the templates".

CHAPTER 12

The Saviour Of The Human Race

The genetic storm was predicted to hit the Earth in only three months time. The whole world was a beehive of activity. Trains, buses, boats and planes were commandeered in order to get the vaccines out to the remotest of places. It was the Berlin Air lift on a massive world-wide scale! And P Day came (Pathogenic Day). For two months, the space bacteria fell on the planet. Those who had been vaccinated suffered no ill effects. Those who had refused the vaccine died in only a matter of days. When the worst was over and the Earth emerged from the pathogenic cloud, Professors Brigmore and Durking were the heroes of the hour. However, everyone from the highest to the lowest wanted to know exactly how they had hit on this miraculous vaccine – for that is what the media termed it. It was arranged that the leaders of the world's nations would assemble at the Ural Research Base, the nerve centre of the entire operation, where the two professors would reveal all.

On the big day, Brigmore and Durking stood in front of over 300 kings, queens, cardinals, presidents and prime ministers. Hundreds of cameras were trained on the massive platform from which Brigmore and Durking were to give their address. The ceremony began with the Czar of Russia welcoming all the high dignitaries from around the world and thanking them for gracing his country with their presence. After the formalities had been dispensed with, Professor William Brigmore was invited by the Russian Minister of Health to talk to the entire world.

"Your Imperial Majesty, Your Majesties, Excellencies: I am most honoured to address this highly distinguished gathering. Our Earth has passed through one of the worst genetic storms in its history, a type of genetic invasion which, millions of years ago, ended the rule of the dinosaurs and almost ended the rule of the human species a mere two months ago. There is no need for me to give a chronological account of the crisis out of which the Earth has just emerged for you are all aware of its ferocious nature. So I shall pass on to an explanation of the events which led to the discovery of the vaccine which saved mankind from extinction.

It all started with a bout of swearing on my part. Frustrated over the adverse consequences related to the original vaccine, I used that most common of curse words 'bloody hell'! It then dawned on me that a year previously a young first year student at Manchester University had told me that we are saved by the Blood of Christ. I confess that I arrogantly and unfairly dismissed her comments. I then decided to initiate approaches to the Vatican . Now the rest of this will astonish you all. I arranged to meet Pope Pius XIII in order to request him to give me samples of the Holy Shroud of Turin which are stained with blood – to many believers, myself now included – the Blood of Jesus Christ. His Holiness kindly and graciously allowed me to take some cuttings from the Shroud back to England with me. I gave these to my colleague Professor Durking whom I will now ask to continue the narrative of these most exciting and most extraordinary events."

Brigmore sat down and the Russian Minister of Health invited Professor Durking to take centre-stage.

"Thank you Professor Brigmore. Like my colleague Professor Brigmore, I also feel highly privileged to speak to such a distinguished audience this day. Well, at first, I must admit, I thought that Professor Brigmore's idea was wild in the extreme, but, we had to give it a try. When the pieces of cloth from the Shroud were safely ensconced in my laboratory at Oxford University , I immediately liquefied the blood on them and, with my research team, established their DNA configuration. Over the past few years, my colleagues and I have been working on a technique to create artificial DNA based upon real DNA templates. It is precisely this technique that we used to make artificial DNA from the Shroud's blood stains. If the man on the Shroud is really Jesus Christ and if the blood is truly His, then, we assumed, that such holy blood and holy DNA would surely be the antidote to the appalling effects of the original vaccine serum. We took a gamble. It was a last desperate try, but in real life I have often found that these last desperate tries are often the ones that pay off. I am sure that I am speaking for the world when I say, I am very glad that this one did".

The following year, Professor William Brigmore went into retirement with not only a Nobel Prize but with a knighthood. Professor John Durking also received these honours and continued his researches into the manufacture of artificial DNA. Professor Brigmore had this to say in his acceptance speech during the Nobel award ceremony:

"No-one now can doubt that many pathogens are extraterrestrial in their origins. The genetic storm through which the Earth passed a year ago will not be the last one – be assured of that. However, we have made astonishing scientific progress since it was established that pathogens hit the Earth from space, yet it is all just a beginning. We need constant vigilance. Research and development must be constantly updated. It is my hope that a new branch of medicine will be opened up – astromedicine. I ask for funds to be made available from both public and private organisations to provide the means by which all levels of the Earth's atmosphere are constantly surveyed in order to detect any incoming pathogenic material. I do not mean to alarm you, but I really must say that the next swarm of pathogens may be even more virulent that the previous one. We cannot rest on our laurels and presume that the Blood from the Turin Shroud will be the cure-all for every space pathogen that hits the Earth. It may be – but it may not be. My belief is that we were given a respite. I firmly believe that we are now in an interregnum period where we must apply tremendous efforts in the way of identifying cosmic pathogens, working out their DNA structures and devising appropriate vaccines in order to counter them. Although officially I have retired, I have only retired from my job – but I have by no means retired from my work, and even less so have I retired from life. It is my intention to spend my retirement years as busily and as productively as I spent my working years. And, needless really to say, my retirement years - or more exactly and more accurately I should term them my *official* retirement years - will be devoted to identifying and analysing space viral and bacterial matter. In conclusion I would like to point out that what for far too long was considered to be in the twilight zone of science is now well ensconced in the mainstream of research and analyses. What was once so unorthodox is now scientific orthodoxy. But, as Sir Fred Hoyle said last century, it is only when we break free of orthodox ways of proceeding and into original modes of thinking that any progress can be made in the realm of science. If the scientific establishment had been more open-minded and had at least given the space pathogens theory a fair chance great progress could have been made in eliminating Aids, Sars, Bird Flu and Swine Flu and so many other flues which caused so many deaths over the last hundred or so years. All of these had their origins in space. How sad that that is only now being recognised.

CHAPTER 13

Haven't We Met Somewhere Before?

When the pathogenic storm had come to an end and the emergency programme of vaccination had been wound up, mankind then began the task of picking up the pieces. Around one quarter of the world's population had been decimated by the bacteria. "Never again" was the resounding message that came from the governments of every single nation on the planet. But that "never again" had to be put into practical effect. Although Sir William Brigmore was supposed to be retired he found himself busier than ever engaged in helping various scientific establishments both in Britain and in other nations with the tasks of setting up programmes for detecting space pathogens and in working out how the new academic discipline of astromedicine would be constituted both in terms of its structure and function. One morning, while he was working in his office at Jodrell Bank, his secretary came to inform him that he had a visitor.

"Who is it Miss Clark?", Brigmore asked.

"The lady did not give me her name", the secretary replied.

"Very well, show her into my office please Miss Clark".

"Yes, Sir William".

A minute later a lady of superb proportions walked into Brigmore's office. Brigmore could not see her face very clearly as extending from the hat she was wearing was a veil that covered most of her face.

"Do you remember me, Professor Brigmore?", asked the mysterious lady.

Somewhat puzzled Brigmore said, "Your voice sounds somewhat familiar – but, I can't quite place you".

"Try Professor, try", said the lady in pleading tones.

"Madam", began Brigmore rather impatiently, "I'm a very busy man and I don't really have time for indulging in guessing games."

The lady then placed her hands at the bottom of the veil which partially covered her face and lifting it, draped it over the top of her hat.

"Dr. Feodora Kostkri", exclaimed Brigmore. "What an unexpected and most pleasant surprise. You are most very welcome".

Brigmore and Kostkri spent the next hour catching up on each other's news. It had been a year since they had been at the Ural Mountains base.

"So what, may I ask, brings you to Manchester ?", Brigmore enquired of his guest.

"I'm here to resume my work in setting up the joint British/Russian Biological Research Laboratories. Two years ago, the space pathogen crisis interrupted progress in setting up this institution and my work had to be diverted to research with the international team in the Urals for finding a way of dealing with the space pathogens".

"I thought you worked for Moscow University ".

" Moscow University is involved in the project and I have been seconded to help in the establishment of the BRBRL".

"You know, I've never heard of this establishment."

"It's been kept rather hush hush until now."

"Why is that?"

"We don't want animal rights protestors trying to sabotage the operation, that's why. Would you like to come and see around the premises?"

"Yes I would. How about tomorrow if that is convenient for you?"

"Tomorrow is just fine. In fact, Professor, this is more than just a courtesy visit. I'm really here to ask you if you would be willing to co-operate with us in adapting our mode of research so that more of our time and facilities would be made available to astromedicine research and the development of techniques for the speedy decoding of alien bacteria and the development of vaccines to counter any diseases from space".

"I'd be very happy to co-operate with you".

The following day, Feodora showed Brigmore around the new research laboratories. After the tour Brigmore told Feodora how impressed he was with the state-of-the-art equipment housed in the premises.

"Would you like to have lunch somewhere Feodora?", said Brigmore. "There's a nice Italian place not far from here. Do you like Italian food or would you prefer somewhere else?"

"Italian food is one of my favourites", Feodora replied. "But first I want to walk by the university car park".

"That's in the opposite direction to *Leonardo's*", Brigmore explained.

"There is a reason for going there".

"Is your car parked there?"

"No! I don't have a car".

"But then why…?

"Just wait and see Professor", interrupted Feodora.

Brigmore and Feodora walked in silence for the five minutes it took them to get to the car park.

"I want you to come over to this spot here Professor", said Feodora.

The two walked over to the place which Feodora had indicated.

"There is no vehicle here Feodora".

"Don't you remember something about this exact spot, Professor?"

"No. Why? Should I? It looks rather ordinary and unimposing".

"Well, Professor it has a significance".

"Feodora. Just put me out of my misery. I have no idea what you are on about."

Feodora looked at Brigmore and smiled a pitying smile.

"Professor Brigmore. It was here that I first me t you – two years ago".

"What *are* you talking about Feodora? I first met you at the Ural base in Russia ".

"Wrong, Professor. It was here – on this very spot".

Brigmore looked curiously at her.

"Look at me Professor! Listen! Are you saved? It is by the Blood of Christ that we are saved".

Brigmore took one pace back and stood agape as he stared at Feodora.

"My God!", exclaimed Brigmore. "So it was *you*. But – I thought, I thought it was a first year student…how?"

"You only saw me for less than a minute. And when I'm off duty and more casually dressed, perhaps I look young enough to pass for a first year undergraduate".

"Well, I'll be damned!", said a completely bowled over Brigmore. "But why didn't you tell me all this when we met in Russia ?"

"It was neither the time nor the place to do it. And in any case, maybe you can answer my question now".

"First of all Feodora, I must apologise for giving you such short shrift on that occasion. And now to answer your question: yes, I am saved by the Blood of Christ in two ways – physically and spiritually. I had no idea that your comment would have had such a profound impact – not only for me but for the entire human species".

"Neither did I Professor. Neither did I. How could anyone have foreseen such a play-out of events from such an off-the-cuff comment. The Lord truly works in mysterious ways."

"This humble spot in this humble car park will be forever to me the most sacred place in the Universe. Now Feodora, let's have that lunch at *Leonardo's.*"

EPILOGUE

Glory be to Jesus,
who in bitter pains
poured for me the life blood
from his sacred veins!

Grace and life eternal
in that blood I find,
blest be his compassion
infinitely kind!

Blest through endless ages
be the precious stream
which from endless torment
doth the world redeem!

There the fainting spirit
drinks of life her fill;
there, as in a fountain,
laves herself at will.

Abel's blood for vengeance
pleaded to the skies;
but the blood of Jesus
for our pardon cries.
Oh the Blood of Christ
It sooths the Father's ire
Opes the Gate of Heaven
Saves from hell's great fire

Oft as it is sprinkled
on our guilty hearts,
Satan in confusion
terror-struck departs;

oft as earth exulting
wafts its praise on high,
angel hosts, rejoicing,
make their glad reply.

Lift ye then your voices;
swell the mighty flood;
louder still and louder
praise the precious blood.

Table of Contents
Space Shanties

SPACE SHANTIES

WE HAVE MADE CONTACT
MESSAGE TRANSMITTED

We have detected your wobble, we think it's a planet
And located within your solar system's habitable zone
So we send you lots of data and scribbles about us
Confident we are not in this vast Universe alone
But part of life's great cosmic tapestry so rich and varied.

Our sun is a main sequence yellow
dwarf star in the location of Orion
Our planet is fourth out of fourteen and
made up of nitrogen and oxygen
It's about seven thousand miles in diameter and
spins on its 23 degree axis
Once ever 27 hours – oh and we have
four seasons seven billion ladies and men
Overpopulated perhaps but it's a matter of political
opinion and standard of living.

We call ourselves 'human beings'- two eyes,
two ears a nose a mouth
Two arms, two legs, five fingers, five toes
and we do suffer from in-growing toenails
And smoking is a problem and so is
passive smoking and drinking past hours

Social problems in the regions of our planet
called the 'first world' and garden snails
Decimating our vegetable patches but
minor problems to those in the 'third world'.

Football, basketball and a variety of sports
and hobbies all help when it comes
To relieving the tensions built up by
a hard week's work but oh to come home
To a nagging wife and screaming bairns
it drives me up the wall you know
And politicians of different parties and religious
evangelicals in our streets roam
Looking for votes and converts and wondering
if we're saved and who gets into power.

We all have our problems washing machine's
broken stock market's fallen
Money devalued and hyperinflation unemployment
and mass immigration
From the poorer parts of our planet
to the richer parts and that causes problems
We've passed through our Industrial Revolution
and now it's quite a sensation
To enter the scientific digital computer age of rockets
and bamboozling technology.

We've visited both our moons and sent rockets
and robots to seven of our nearest neighbours all
uninhabited except for Tarel the fifth planet
its got plants and trees
And there are some who say it's a waste of money

as there are poor people here
So we should close down astronomy
and space research: Why? Why? the keys
To our future are out there in space opening doors
to goodness know where.

The Reply

What a surprise what a surprise now we know there's life
Apart from our own in this universe so vast
We're the twentieth planet cast
In Alpha Centaur's binary system rife
With planets moons comets asteroids and meteorites.

Alpha Centauri is made up of two stars
Each star has its own set of planets
But an outer plane of planets
Orbits both stars
That's where we are twentieth out of thirty five.

Two suns - boy oh boy that's hot
If like you we were fourth in line
That would not be fine
For life to evolve it would not
But be roasted and sizzled and cooked.

So our habitable zone is way out nearer the edge
We've got our solar system all to ourselves
Each of our astronomers delves
Into the Universe and often allege
At last signs of life – but false alarm until now.

Yet your info is a bit disappointing
And we'll probably disappoint you
We're exactly the same as you
Polluted rivers fewer birds on the wing

Teenage pregnancies single parent families – y'know!

If you really want data on us
We'll just take what you sent and in haste
Click, copy, paste
Send – no more there's a computer virus and damn I've
to catch a bus
Private transport's been banned oil reserves near
depletion.

REPLY FROM ORION

Ah yes it is somewhat disappointing
we expected weird monsters
And gooey things with three eyes that could fly
and transform themselves
Well at least that's what our science fiction writers
imagined and wrote about
So that's what we all believed about "aliens"
and "extraterrestrials" but you're like us
We dream we scheme we take showers
and go to the cinema to watch Lone Star.

But what are those things some on our planet
report seeing in the sky?
We call them UFOs or flying saucers –
disk shaped things and some people
Even claim to be abducted by them
and report that their occupants have bulbous
Heads and large glaring eyes and perform
operations on them and stick wires up their
Oh!! I won't say it – but most of us think it's pie
in the sky and a downright lie.

Strange mysteries like crop circles who built the
pyramids and ghostly apparitions
Out of the body experiences on the surgeon's table
but I say it's all neurological
Tricks of the mind and a boot up the behind
will bring these people down to Breeathem

(Oh bye the way that's the name of our planet at least in the Camana language there are millions of languages on our planet) and cure them of their irrational superstitions.

Say! What do you call your planet well at least in the language of your particular nation?

REPLY FROM ALPHA CENTAURI

We call our planet Phenlizha it must sound funny
to but you the strange phenomenon
Of unidentified flying machines is something we
experience too and we blamed it
On people living on other planets but
we give it the same rational explanation as you
But with the addition of a combination
of hallucinogens and New Age Philosophy
The sort long haired louts and the 'peace man'
brigade all subscribe to - a real con.

We have a TV series called Doctor Hoo
and it features weird and wonderful robots
And computers and things that come to life
and take over the world and then the Universe
And Doctor Hoo saves the Universe
and then the world from these metallic machines
Well the kids like it it gives them a scare
but they can't wait until the next thrilling
Episode when Doctor Hooey saves the Universe
and the world in the same time slots.

But if this isn't all just a load of old phony baloney
and these things really exist
Where exactly are they located in the galactic
scheme of things? Do you have any idea?
Perhaps the Universe has an underlying pattern
which makes us all carbon copies

Of carbon based life which culminates in upright two-
legged humans and the underlying
Pattern for the Doctor Hoo monsters are in the
collective cosmic imagination's mist.

Rudely Interrupted

Pardon us gentlemen but we are from the most
advanced nation on Stlana a planet
In the habitable zone of Betelgeuse so we're one
hundredth from this giant gannet
Of a star that eats anything that gets too close we've
been eavesdropping on you
So we know all about crop circles venereal diseases
and this Doctor Hooey
We're human like you part of the cosmic pattern
slight variation we have Doctor Phooey.

Now we shan't bore the pants off you
by telling you of our own social goo
That affects us as much as it affects you two too
and that would add to our feeling of blue
So we'd like to postulate a theory about
this underlying cosmic structure
That it extends to our social goo
and true to say it lurks sure
In a flaw in this universal pattern a tear
in a curtain a tear in the eye a tare to allure
The field to produce cockle but not the true crops
of a good and wholesome manure.

From Breeathem And Phenlizha to Stlana

So what exactly is your theory
Dearie?
We are leery
Of another eerie
Theory
Which aims to query
Established theory
That makes us weary
My dearie.

From Stlana To Breeathem And Phenlizha

Here we're one step ahead of the game
than you two planets so listen up
We have been picking up all the electronic buzz
from a planet of a star
We call Mnenna it is located in the same
spiral arm of the galaxy in which
Our star systems are located this planet is third from
Mnenna and we simply have labeled it X3P10001 as
we're running out of names
for all the extra solar planets we've found.

Men had been on X3P10001 for long but one day the
God of the Universe decided
To breathe a soul into a human he named Adam and
his wife Eve so Adam was the first human made in
the image of God but his wife Eve soon ate of the
forbidden fruit of a forbidden tree and sin and death
and imperfection descended upon that planet.
All X3P10001ians were kept from the paradise of the
afterlife by this mistake.

From Breeathem And Phenlizha To Stlana

Surely it only condemns that planet to all this woe
Why does it affect us so
Why should we go
To Hell for a foe
We do not know?

From Stlana To Breeathem And Phenlizha

As Adam's sin affected all humanity on X3P10001 so it
affects humanity
In the entire Universe so Breeathemians, Phenlizhias
and Stlananians
Are all cursed by this disobedience of one man and one
woman and all
Must suffer and die and be condemned to some vile
underworld far from Heaven?

FROM BREEATHEM AND PHENLIZHA TO STLANA

Here is the explanation our species
has waited for so long
Yet has never been able to work out –
nay not even the best of our philosophers
But what is the solution? How do we right
the wrongs? How do we return
To Eden and Paradise and a world
or rather worlds free from despair?

FROM STLANA TO BREEATHEM AND PHENLIZHA

Two thousand years ago according
to X3P10001's time reckonings
God Incarnate in the Person of Jesus Christ
came to X3P10001
As Saviour Messiah and Redeemer
and suffered and died on
A cross and that whoever believes
this will be saved from damnation.

From Stlana, Breeathem and Phenlizha To X3P10001

So now we've told you all about us tell us all about you
And tell us more about your religion true
And the Saviour of the world and the Universe do not tarry
We need very quickly your missionary.

From X3P10001 to Stlana, Breeathem and Phenlizha

Oh you boys are a bore
We don't believe all that any more
Religion now ain't so terrific
We've gone ever so scientific.

We get our highs on alcohol and drugs
Religion and that oh that's for mugs
Whatever your class is - come
It's opium for the masses rather than Masses
opprobrium.

Some folks on this planet (oh we call it Earth in
English) are still spiritual
And in front of altar and clergy crawl
As for me I gotta go now so no more
I've got an appointment with my regular whore.

From Valmana To X3P10001, Stlana, Breeathem and Phenlizha

We've been listening into you three's messages –
what an uproar
And we are of your science fiction lore
Cybermen, Daleks, ice-warriors,
programmed robots with a laser gun
But we're more human than the humans on X3P10001.

We're not a nice lot women wouldn't be at all turned on
Ask them for a dance and we'd be told to be gone
Our good looks our charms our finesse rather few
Our creator was Doctor Goodness Knows Who.

We suffer from megalomania,
egoism and loads of vanity
But we can teach you the rudiments of Christianity
So when He comes to X3P10001 in a century or eleven
There will be more Valmanians, Stlananians,
Breeathemians and Phenlizhanains than X3P10001ians
in Heaven.

And who in Heaven for all eternity should reign
A Dalek standing before the Lamb that was slain.

CINATIT

They said it was indestructible designed
to withstand oncoming meteorites
Space debris and asteroids that could not
penetrate its hyper-tensile steel
So Captain Gung Ho gave the order for
full speed through the asteroid belt
Our ship will heavy and elbow them out
of the way he said over potatoes and veal.

Oh Captain Gung Ho look at that
massive asteroid ahead we must change course
There will be a collision and the ship
will be wrecked but no no Gung Ho
Would have none of it no maneuver
no circuitous route go gung ho
Said Gung Ho then crash smash boom
we've hit it oh no oh yes Gung Ho.

Captain Gung Head realised his mistake
but it was too late there just weren't
Enough life ships for all the passengers
and crew so the lucky few could wait
Until rescue came from the colonies on
Mars but that would take a while
The rest had to stay on the poor wrecked ill fated
Cinatit - spell it backwards.

The engines went dead and the ship had a leak

and the dangerous cosmic rays
Started to slowly but surely fill up the ship the rays
came in and the oxygen seeped out
And everyone started to cough and choke and
hallucinate about being rescued
By NASA life-crafts or failing that by any altruistic
aliens that might be around.

Being more imaginative than the rest
I put on a pressure suit and jumped overboard
And started to swim through space lucky for me
the atmosphere on the asteroid
The same one that smacked us was breathable
but it was inhabited by aliens
And I asked them if they could whisk me
back to Earth or Mars would be just fine.

They weren't very happy about being hit
by our ship they never considered
Their asteroid as indestructible so why
were we so arrogant and cock sure
About our ship Oh I'm not the captain
and I did warn the silly clot
All right we'll transport you back to Earth
but you'll have to work your passage.

Go down the mines of this asteroid
and dig up the ore we work here you know
This is not an asteroid holiday resort and
if you don't work we'll make you
Walk the plank into space without a space suit
and oxygen cylinder

So make your choice oh I'll work down the mines
and bring out the ore.

At last they took me back to Earth but
on the return journey I had to cook
My own breakfast and other meals and theirs too so I
dished out the bacon and eggs
And so often I heard get the tomato sauce
and a bit more chili pepper over here
They dropped me on Earth on the White House lawn
with a frying pan of bacon and eggs.

MUTINY ON THE BOUNTIFUL

Planet Zogulgulon had a species of plant
Of which the Space Federation so often did rant
Purple not green they were a great prize
For these plants never photosynthesise.

Captain Plyers of the Bountiful was told to come
To Zogulgulon for the plant species called Boozulum
Bring loads of them back they may be good
And solve the Earth's problem about its food.

So Plyers and crew they got to Zogulgulon
And started pulling up Boozulum by the tonulum
Excuse me captain a thousand pardons
But Bountiful looks more and more like Kew Gardens .

Plyers then hollered I don't give a stuff
Look after these plants and feed them enough
And to help these plants I'll tell you what
Your own food rations are now to be cut.

These plants are not used to very much light
So on the return journey of this flight
Wear constant night goggles for to me hark
The Bountiful will be constantly dark.

If there's too much light then this I surmise
The plants will start to photosynthesise
Get sick and go green with high chlorophyll rates
And vomit up into the pudding plates.

Oh Captain Plyers you are so cruel
We cannot possibly survive on gruel
We mutiny we're taking over this ship
And overboard you we're going to tip.

Get into that life craft near the berth
That should get you back to Earth
We'll settle on a nearby planet we've seen
Flowing with water and plants that are green.

What am I going to eat? asked the captain
Those pants we'll put some in a bin
Have them with coffee and your tea
Goodbye now captain and bon appetite

When the captain returned the Earth was breezy
But oh he felt so awfully queasy
The Federation Chairman turned and said
Captain you're all purple, violet and red!

The Federation Committee they tried the Boozulum
But they got indigestion in their tumulum
A headache to boot oh they weren't in clover
The Boozulum plant massively hung over em.

THE MARY CELESTIAL

We saw the space ship flying between Jupiter and Mars
We radioed them – no answer. Need any help?
Are you OK?
Still no answer. So the captain decided we should
send over a boarding party.

Deserted!! Yet everything is functioning normally.
Transmitters and engines OK
And there's a pot of scotch broth still quite warm.
But where are the crew? the
Life craft are still there. This is very strange
there's no explanation.

We'll take this ship with us back to Earth
but first let's not waste that good soup
So on the return journey we tried to solve the mystery
Which we all agreed would go down in history.

A ghost space ship – where had the crew gone?
Were they spirited away by aliens?
Had they found the meaning of life?
Had they discovered the "whys" of the Universe?
Did they get caught in a time vortex? They could have
been smuggling asteroid mined gems.

But how do you explain the fact that the life craft were
still there? Perhaps some space monster beamed in and
ate them all up. Oh don't be such a Silly Billy, there are
no such thing as space monsters.

We went to the ship's owners and we
thought we'd done well in bringing back
Their *Mary Celestial.* We were beaming
with smiles but they were frosty and cold
Look here is the captain of the
Mary Celestial and all of the crew.

You nincompoops! Why did you interfere
with our fully automated space ship?
You busybodies have wrecked our experiments.
There never was anyone on board
The *Mary Celestial.* In fact there was
never meant to be anyone on board.

Oh so sorry we thought we did well
and imagined that it would save you
Hikes in your space insurance premiums
and maintain your no claims bonuses
You said the *Mary Celestial* was empty
while you did fume and froth
But pray tell us – how do you explain
the warm scotch broth?

A Space Battle

The Admiral walked space suited
on the deck while the battle raged
And a sniper from one of the alien's ships
with which we were engaged
Fired a laser at the Admiral down he fell and so
We took him mortally wounded below.

I want the First Officer said the Admiral
please tell him to hurry
He's fighting a Klingon but here's his robot
to see you don't worry
Oh well if he's going to be sloppy and tardy
Then electronically digitally kiss me Hardy.

SPACEABIANCA

The boy stood on the radiation deck
Whence all but he had fled
The laser that lit the battle's wreck
Radiated round him the aliens said.

Though glowing bright just there he stood
In ferocious cosmic storm
A creature of uranium inflected blood
It mangled up his form.

The beams rolled on, he would not go
Without his computer's word
That computer full of virus below
Its commands no longer heard.

He called aloud "Say, computer, say
If yet my programme's done"
He knew not that the laptop lay
Unconscious of this one.

"Speak computer", once again he cried
"If I may yet be gone"
And but the blooming error messages replied
And fast the beams rolled on.

Radiation beams and a laser ray
Where is the boy please say?
Somewhere in space with his atoms he sits
And his computer's algorithmic bits.

OF MEN AND GALAXIES
(FORTY FIVE YEARS ON)

Sir Fred Hoyle gave a series of lectures at the University of Washington in 1964. In 1961, John and Jesse Danz made a substantial gift to the University of Washington to establish a fund to provide income to be used to bring to the university each year "….distinguished scholars of national and international reputation who have concerned themselves with the impact of science and philosophy on man's perception of a rational universe. It was as a "John Danz Lecturer" that Hoyle spoke at the University of Washington in 1964. The central question of this essay is "how does *Of Men And Galaxies* relate to the present day (2009)?" We shall examine the issues brought up by Hoyle in 1964 and compare and contrast them with the current era.

It is interesting to note that in the first of those lectures Hoyle made the comment that "Everything radically new is always produced in a democracy". And – "…the people of a dictatorship are inherently less ingenious than the people of a democracy". The context in which Hoyle made these, I would say, perfectly accurate observations, was the production of the nuclear bomb. It was the democracies, not the dictatorships which produced it – not out of any moral decision on the part of the latter, but because of this lesser degree of inherent genius.

Let us put Hoyle's comments into another and more contemporary context – the current on-going attempts to build a European super-state. What then is the future for native European national genius and inventiveness if the construction of this undemocratic mega-state gathers momentum and reaches its apogee in a massive structure in which governance is essentially conducted on the basis of diktat and decree? Not a very promising one surely. Europe is going to be left lagging behind America and the rest of what will be by then "the free world".

In the field of science, Hoyle pointed out that the groundwork for the great scientific discoveries of the second thirty years of the twentieth century was laid in the first thirty years of that century – and that these discoveries were made with equipment which cost only hundreds of dollars. Between 1954 and 1964, the best three or four discoveries in physics were made with very simple equipment. Since then the cost of scientific equipment has run into the hundreds and even the thousands of millions of dollars. A large piece of scientific apparatus not only costs more to construct but is slower to construct, thus the rate of scientific breakthrough is inevitably greatly slowed down.

Hoyle did not accept the inevitability of these massive machines as the means of procuring more and greater scientific discoveries. He called this way of thinking "the dinosaur mentality" but he felt confident that it would come to an end "…. Partly because it is in the nature of dinosaurs to reach an end, to become extinct". Ever bigger machines cannot, he argued, be built without a limit, "…. if only because this activity cannot consume more than the total energy of the whole human species."

But Hoyle explained that there is no need to despair. He directed the thoughts of his audience towards his own specialties – astronomy and astrophysics. He invited his listeners to "Think of the whole universe as a laboratory" as within stars the properties of matter are subject to conditions "…that can never be simulated in a (terrestrial) laboratory." He predicted that there would be a shift in the balance of experimentation made in the earthly laboratory and in what he termed "the universal laboratory" – a shift in favour of the latter. Perhaps the Hubble telescope is an example of Hoyle's prediction being vindicated, for relative to its size (though large and expensive) it has accumulated information that would have taken over a hundred years and many more times its cost to gain the information it collected in around fifteen years of life.

So when the highly philosophical question is asked about the purpose of the universe, the Christian can answer that it is "God's laboratory" put at the disposal of Man. It is ironical that we can come to this conclusion on the observation of an atheist. Indeed God works in mysterious ways!

Hoyle then extends this analysis of the scientific method to the wider aspects of life. Just as when the scientist becomes more bogged down in detail and minutiae his capacity for original thought and discovery becomes stunted, so does the large building, office, or organisation overawe those who work in them into a state of rigid conformity and, consequently, rigid modes of thought and procedure. "The old free and easy conditions have gone, the sort of conditions I remember when as a student in Cambridge , thirty years ago, I used to tiptoe past Rutherford 's laboratory. We now have vast, slick, streamlined laboratories, more reminiscent of an industrial production plant than of a laboratory in the old sense." "….laboratories cannot be shut down for four or five days while one goes off on a fishing trip in the mountains. The trouble is that it is the fishing trips that lead to the big ideas….. Maxwell, Planck, Einstein, Rutherford – none of these men depended on big science, they depended on big ideas." Hoyle explained that big facilities cost money, and the obtaining of financial grants depends upon lobbying . The result is that scientists spend less time doing science and more time engaged in committees, lobbying and the giving of press conferences. A very interesting observation made by Hoyle was that no-where in the world was any great scientist to be found in the inner councils of government. Whilst many scholars in law, economics and the arts find their way into politics, no major scientist has ever done so. Hoyle put this down to the fact that generally, scientists are content just to be scientists. Unfortunately, governments will herd scientists into committees and other bureaucratic bodies so as to pick their brains on a number of issues –

most notably on military defence systems. Hoyle saw it as scandalous that half a scientist's working life should be spent in this non-research, non-productive capacity. He saw it is part and parcel of the mistaken belief that people are at their best in their youth. In arts and music "…. The proposition is not true. In fact the reverse is true; the best work is frequently produced in later years." He claimed that the relation between age and quality of work is cultural – "The insidious presumption is that a good man can afford some loss of time…". Hoyle believed that it was this presumption that does the damage.

Perhaps today we would call this "the cult of youth". Youthful vigour has been focused on to such a narrow extent that we have become oblivious to the experience and wisdom that can only come with age and the " University of Life ".

Hoyle noted that at birth we are equipped to live in any kind of society – even the most primitive kind and "… to accept any social convention, however absurd." But by the time we are twenty, this ability to adapt and change ceases, we are stuck in our ways and fully conformed to the society we have grown up in. This observation I believe could be applied to the present day phenomenon of mass immigration and its attendant philosophy of multiculturalism. Immigrants having been culturally formed in one particular society are not going to be capable of adapting to the host society. I am not sure what Sir Fred Hoyle's views on this hot topic were, or even if he ever expressed any, and I'm not sure if he would have approved of my using his words within a discussion and analysis of this highly contentious political subject, but the comparison is not way off reasonable limits and the analogy is close and rational.

Hoyle finished the first of his three lectures by warning against efficiency. "Beware of efficiency….It seems to be characteristic of all great work in every field, that it arises spontaneously and unpretentiously, and that its creators wear a cloak of imprecision…..It is the man with the flashy air of knowing everything, who is always on the ball, always with it, that we should beware of. It will not be very long now before his behaviour can be imitated quite perfectly by a computer." This last statement of Hoyle's shows him to be years ahead of the time in which he was speaking. While computers can be super-efficient and calculate in a way that leaves the human brain streets behind, they cannot come up with original thoughts and bright ideas. People like Newton , Mozart and Einstein, were regarded as vague, impractical and scatterbrained – yet look at their achievements, achievements which their detractors can never match. And it would seem to me that as long as computers are our masters instead of vice versa, the original thoughts and great ideas will never be realised. We do not have to wait until computers have reached a greater level of sophistication before they have the ability to run amuck; as long as we cannot tear ourselves away from our keyboards and think beyond the confines of our monitors, then we are no more imaginative than the contraption in front of us – man and machine have already become indistinguishable. But surely if we make the worthwhile effort to engage in lateral and imaginative thinking, then computers, no matter what their level of sophistication may be, will always be our servants rather than our masters. It is up to us. And I firmly believe that it boils down to basically this – we have to respect ourselves as human beings. If we don't, how can we expect machines to?!

Hoyle opened the second of his lectures by considering the possibility of creating an artificial human being. He conjectured that cells could be synthesised and fitted together to create a human being. Hoyle asked the question as to whether there would be any recognisable difference between a real human and an artificial one. He concluded by stating that "Chemical similarity may not be sufficient to guarantee similarity of behaviour....." He elucidated this by explaining that "....the same kind of atom in the same kind of arrangement need not behave identically, because the state of the atom is also relevant." This also applies to molecules, and in an even more complex way than atoms. Only if all the atoms and molecules in the artificial man were put together in the correct state would the artificial man and the naturally born man be the same. So making an artificial living being is far more complicated than simply putting the right atoms and molecules in the right order.

And here we have an issue which Hoyle did not touch upon in his lecture – atheistic science (particularly evolutionary theory) asks us to accept that the vast complexity of life is all the product of chance. Careful, conscious and methodological techniques cannot produce an artificial man exactly like the real man, yet blind chance can! Hoyle poses the question – "How much information is required to specify even the simplest single cell? More than is required for a nuclear reactor or an oil refinery, more perhaps than for a star. Yet all the information is contained in a cell no more than a few tens of millionths of an inch in size – the nucleic acid, or DNA as the familiar term has it." And this is only the simplest cell – yet the vast complexity of life on earth is supposed to have "just happened" and evolved blindly.

Hoyle spoke about the possibility of intelligent life elsewhere in the galaxy and the possibility of communicating with it. Because of the vast distances, he believed that deep space travel would never be possible, but communication by use of radio and picture transmissions would be the way of "getting to know you". In fact, Hoyle stated that it would be better for civilisations not to mix so as to preserve the many cultures in the galaxy. And here I would risk again Hoyle's displeasure by applying his thesis to the terrestrial polemic of culture vs. multiculturalism (or rather – non-culture). What would apply in a galactic sense would surely apply in a terrestrial sense – cultures should not mix if they wish to preserve themselves and so provide for a truly multi-cultural world.

In the third and final lecture, Hoyle spoke about the problems of growing world population and the effect this was having on the aesthetic quality of human life. The number of places where one can "get away from it all" are becoming ever fewer. He saw the greatest goal of people in the developed world was to achieve status. In a poor country, people will work simply to survive. As economic prosperity increases, people will want to acquire luxuries. "Once you can afford everything, nothing seems really worthwhile any more. In the present day world, there still remains leisure. But leisure, solitude, absence of noise and racket are all on the way out. One thing remains however – status." However, those not of an atheistic frame of mind would say that there is religion. Christians would look to find ways of serving Christ and his Church better.

A truly Christian mindset would realise that luxuries and status will eventually go the way of all flesh and thus all that would really be of any importance at all are the treasures which the Christian had built up in Heaven.

Hoyle makes a comparison between large and small communities: "A great deal has been written about the narrowness of the small community, much of it not very well judged in my opinion. It is true that the literary man, the intellectual, may find the atmosphere of such a community stifling to his inventive powers. He will feel the urge to be away to the big city. But to most people the small community supplies the readiest fulfillment of our natural craving for social approbation. This craving has played a completely necessary part in the development of civilisation, from its first crude beginnings in village and tribal communities up to the present day." This seems to dovetail with Hoyle's analysis and critique of modern day scientific methods and procedures which he saw as damaging to the chances of making any real progress in scientific research and development. The small community, he contended, "....still acts as the spur for much of the inventiveness of those who work creatively , whether in the humanities or the sciences." So it is not only the size of the workplace and the size of the equipment that are being used that can be stifling to the human intellect and human inventiveness, but the size of the communities in which we live would seem to have some bearing on these and other human qualities. "....what used to be capable of ready fulfillment for everyone is utterly barred in our great cities."

But Hoyle pointed out that no political party has ever fought an election on the real issues connected with this phenomenon "…..increase in privacy, less crowding in cities, smaller communities, and, above all, less pressure in our everyday lives….". He claimed that the reason no political party ever took up these issues was because they are not vote winners. And the reason they are not is correlated to income level: the higher income earners see the problem more clearly because they realise that money will not buy peace, calm and serenity; but the lower orders blame the absence of these on a lack of money. And it is the lower and middle income earners who hold the main voting power. Thus it is, Hoyle concluded, that elections are decided on trivial issues rather than on the real and major issues which affect the entire human species. And there is certainly no evidence today that politicians are anywhere near to even starting to speak about these issues, let alone tackling them. "Increase in privacy" – both at national and supranational level our privacy is being constantly eroded and invaded. We see this particularly in the diktats and decrees of the EU. "Less crowding in the cities" – mass immigration is not only resulting in more overcrowding in the big cities but in the eating up of valuable and indeed beautiful countryside. "Smaller communities" – in fact the combination of the latter two issues makes that impossible. The EU, large scale regional government and such like mammoth structures ensure a remoteness from the people the likes of which have never before been seen. The relationship of the manorial lord and peasant would have been closer and indeed, more democratic than the relationship today between politicians and voters.

It would appear that there is something of a contradiction between Hoyle's preference for village life and small scale science and enterprises on the one hand, and his galactic vision involving contact with extra-terrestrial civilisations on the other. I think not. As already mentioned, Hoyle did not think that these civilisations should mix, as to do so would lead to cultural breakdown. Hoyle spoke about the possibility of intelligent and rational life throughout the galaxy learning from each other through means of a "galactic library". For example, older civilisations than our own might be able to teach us how to avoid nuclear war. They could tell us about the political and social processes that lead up to it.

To see the big picture does not mean that we forget the smaller elements in that picture. A planet is as much composed of atoms as a pin-head is. And in order to know how minute sub-atomic particles work under intense heat and pressure, we have to look to the conditions inside stars and gas clouds. And terrestrial discoveries in the way sub-atomic particles behave have likewise led to a better understanding of the larger extra-terrestrial picture – for example, the discoveries by Bohrs, Heisenberg and Rutherford in the way sub-atomic particles behave (and Rutherford's eventual splitting of the atom to create nuclear energy) have helped scientists understand the nuclear processes within stars. Thus there is an interaction and inter-linkage between the small scale and the large scale, they are not mutually exclusive, and while they do not operate in isolation from each other, their linkage does not result in the cancelling out of one or the other. It is thus reasonable to conclude that smallness no more confers insignificance than largeness confers the opposite quality. Both are connected and interdependent. Narrowness of thought and intellectual myopia occur when there is an over-concentration of focus - whether on a macro or micro level. Parochialism is when the small scale is left unrelated to the larger picture. But a large breadth of vision is blurred and abstracted to the point where it can no longer be defined when its micro component elements are ignored.

Advances in technology over the past forty years have in fact given greater impetus towards smaller scale operations. Hoyle mentioned the digital computer in the first of his lectures, but it was not until 1981 that the first P C came onto the mass market. What once took up massive amounts of room space, now sits on the top of a desk or even in the palm of a human adult hand. Therefore the ability to access information and effect speed of communication no longer requires massive outlay in terms of education, (one does not need a university degree any more to operate a computer) capital investment or space. Cottage industry is once more taking the field again, but it is an electronic cottage industry characterised by such phenomena as digital small scale operations and hyper-computers in the sitting-room whereby this revolution is returning full circle towards pre-industrial revolution type economic production structures - but minus any cranky notions suggestive of a "going back to the caves".

One interesting point Hoyle made was that no-one is a single individual. Each and every one of us is a composite of persons as we are all influenced to one degree or another by many different people. Bearing this in mind, it would be imperative to be careful and selective with regard to whom we are influenced by and whom we model ourselves on – particularly so in the case of the young who tend to gravitate towards the lowest common denominator – drug addicted rock stars and such like.

So, the inevitable question is – have we made any progress as human beings forty-five years on from *Of men and Galaxies*? Far from it is the sad conclusion. In fact, the many problems outlined by Hoyle, far from being effectively tackled, are in fact being reinforced and their ill effects compounded. It was interesting to note that for a non-Christian, Sir Fred Hoyle touched upon one of the most profound of Christian teachings, namely, that money will not buy the things that add quality to life. Hoyle saw nationalism as "a group form of status". Therefore if the good we do our communities gives us status, then as Christians we must redirect that status away from our selfish egos towards increasing the greater status of Almighty God. Give the glory to God and not to ourselves. Let God take the credit and not us. Is there not a connection here between our craving for the big and our rejection of God? I believe there is, for having rejected the True God, we are creating our own gods, our own Golden Calves. We have turned our backs on the True Bigness, to make feeble attempts at creating our own pathetic little "bignesses". It is therefore a great paradox, if we accept this analysis, that it is an atheist scientist who is suggesting, in whatever subliminal way and however vaguely, the Christian solution – although he never mentions it in either Christian or any other religious terms.

Not much has changed between 1964 and 2009; in fact whatever changes there have been, have been for the worse. Will the next forty years be any different? Or will it be more of the same? We simply just don't know. Sir Fred, during these lectures, spoke about the possibility of making contact with other civilisations "out there" and so, by our communications with them, build up a "galactic library". Civilisations older and more advanced than our own could teach us how to avoid nuclear war, was one of the examples given and mentioned above. I have noticed that science fiction films tend to depict planets inhabited with intelligent life as being united under a single government. Sir Fred Hoyle believed that carbon based life would be very similar in structure to earth based life. Thus if biological patterns are similar, so should political ones be, and the reality will be that inhabited planets will be divided into nation states just the same as our Earth is. While we may have to learn from older civilisations, these will be our teachers but not our science fiction gods; our mentors, but not our saviours; they may have more experience than we do, but they will not be super-human. In fact, they will probably have their own science fiction fantasies just the same as we do – but the fantasy will always be fantasy, whether here on Earth or elsewhere. My own fancy is that these older civilisations could teach us not to pooh pooh the nation state; to reject supra-nationalism; to maintain cultural integrity by eschewing mass immigration and multiculturalism; to avoid single currencies and all forms of artificial and unworkable common policies: but above all, they may teach us that turning our back on the Creator and Sustainer of the Universe "in Whom we live, move and have our being", is the greatest mistake of all and the source and root cause of all our ills. But would we be too stubborn and pig-headed to accept this analysis, even from a civilisation greater, older and more advanced than our own.?

A CLOSER EXAMINATION

In *Of Men and Galaxies* Sir Fred Hoyle sees our future evolution as being non-biologically based "…..the environment that determines our evolution is no longer essentially physical". Instead, Hoyle states that "our environment is chiefly conditioned by the things we believe." In order to illustrate this postulation, Hoyle takes two examples – Morocco and California . He notes that "….they are in very similar latitudes, both on the west coasts of continents with similar climates, and probably with rather similar natural resources. Yet their present development is wholly different, not so much because of different people even, but because of different thoughts that exist in the minds of their inhabitants." The main point which Hoyle makes is that "the most important factor in our environment is the state of our own minds."

So the major question then is – what exactly is the difference in the mindset between Moroccans and

Californians? The difference lies between a culture which encourages innovation, inventiveness and change and one which is embedded in a fossilised and unyielding conservatism. More specifically it is the distinction between Christian and Islamic culture. Hoyle states, "we cannot think outside the particular patterns that our brains are conditioned to…" One could well object to this statement on the grounds that (in this particular example) Californians are no less restricted by the thought processes of their particular community. That objection may be countered by Hoyle's observation that "…. we can only think a little way outside, and then only if we are very original". In the case of the inhabitants of California , they have gone that "little way outside" and are thus "very original". That "little way" has made such a big difference. There are many other examples which are even more striking in contrast than the one of Morocco and California . Japan is a country which has virtually no natural or mineral resources, most of its land is volcanic and earthquake prone, yet, next to the United States , it is the wealthiest nation in the world. Its population stands at 120 million. Nations which we refer to as constituting the "third world" are teeming with natural and mineral resources and have low population levels, yet they are poor, backward and underdeveloped. This clearly bears out the thesis that any given country's level of prosperity and state of development begins within the head! Throwing money at these nations in the form of "foreign aid" and "development grants" is not the solution. Cash will simply be spirited away into numbered Swiss bank accounts and development projects will merely add to the stock of inefficient enterprises and so contribute

Francis A. Andrew.

to the crumbling infrastructure. The answer lies in the inhabitants of these third world nations embarking upon a complete overhaul of their mindsets. And this they have to do in their own way and in their own time. Far from doing any good, foreign aid will only serve to confirm these peoples in their obstinate conservatism whereas a cessation by western nations of aid would force the third world into having to reconsider their corrupt practices and thus raise their level of integrity.